# SOLACE VALLEY

MACKENZIE PARSONS

October 7, 2007

Mom's side of the family bickers in the kitchen. Cupboard doors slam open and shut. I'm sitting on a footstool in the living room. Mind's racing. The din makes the walls feel like they're closing in. I want to be anywhere but here. The blinds are closed instead of letting the fall afternoon light in. I'm searching through my phone for movie times. My stomach churns and turns over itself.

"Morgan! Madison!" our aunt screams out from down the hall. Everyone freezes for a moment before running to her voice.

My mind pulls me backwards. My heart moves me forward, knowing what's to come. My spirit floats behind me, pushing me closer.

The hall logjams with family members. I'm almost to the door when another relative tries to shove me aside. I deflect their cold arm and clear the way so my brother and I can make it in. Before another body gets by, I slam the door shut behind us. Time and space are a surreal blur until we're inside the sewing room. Then it all grinds to a halt.

The door shuts behind me. I look to the bed against the wall, hoping with every ounce of my being to prove my gut wrong. It's futile to struggle with what's happening.

My brother and I bolt to our mother's bedside and embrace each other, our aunt, and Mom.

She's hardly recognizable in her state. The cancer's drained her. The tumor in her liver's large enough that she looks pregnant. Though she's been unresponsive the last few days, her body's finally giving out. Her eyes are vacant and hollowly stare at the ceiling. Her chest heaves. Her arms lie stiffly at her sides, legs just as rigid below. She sighs loudly and repeatedly with the hint that each may be her last.

"Don't worry Mom, we'll be alright," Madison assures her along with each of us there.

Mom's head turns to face us. Her gaze cuts directly past us. Her eyes focus, all the while she continues to sigh. Her eyes widen in full and she smiles in wonder, as though she's just seen the most beautiful sight of her life. A wave of peace washes over her face. Her body sinks into the bed and lies still.

"Mom... Mom! MOM!!" I cry out and fall to my knees. Grasping her cold and lifeless hand, I burst into tears. We each do.

I look up to see tears streaming down my brother's and aunt's faces. Milo and Macy, our parents' dogs, lie curled up next to Mom in mourning of their own. Milo whimpers, nudges Mom's shoulder, and sinks next to her, resting his head on her.

The room sways and accelerates into a steady swirl around me. My stomach acid feels as though I'll soon be engulfed. Still holding Mom's hand, I look up at the ceiling light. Flickering slowly at first, then rapidly the more I stare with tear-soaked eyes. Though it's only one in the afternoon, the skies outside darken to a sickly, bitter gray. Lightning dances across the sky. My cries deepen, attempting to rid all the pain and fear from my body. I scream, wishing it might be my own death rattle.

CrackcrackCRACK! A burst of lightning darts in through the window and strikes the light overhead, illuminating it fully before ricocheting down to me. The light blinds me at first, filling my eyes, then courses throughout my body.

The light shatters, causing bolts of light to scream in all directions. Circling around the room, the vortex of light pulls closer as the energy radiates and pulses through me. Enveloping me in a shimmering electric cloud, the light forces every scrap of pain and fear out of me in a final gasp.

Darkness.

In all directions.

Stillness.

Quiet.

Am I dead too?

Thump thump... Thump thump...

A heartbeat.

Mine?

I blink a few times, breathing deeply and scan the room. The light's still intact overhead, no flicker, no signs of a break. The sky outside's a serene blue with no traces of clouds. The window's open with no signs of cracked glass. A breeze glides in and brings my head up. My aunt and brother look down at Mom with tears in their eyes.

Bizarre, that felt like hours had passed by, but must have

only been a few moments. Breathing a sigh of relief, I'm at peace. I'm alive, but how?

I let go of Mom's hand and wipe my forehead. I wipe the tears from my face and pause. What the... I blink a few more times. This can't be right. What am I seeing? Are these my hands? Impossible.

Looking down at both my hands, my jaw drops in disbelief. Flipping each hand over, my stomach lurches again. Tears fill my eyes. Fear consumes me while I try to make sense of what I'm looking at. What happened to me? I glance at my aunt, then Madison to see if they notice me. Nothing.

Fear turns to panic. I've got to stand up and get out of here. I need to hide somewhere alone with Hudson so I can try to make sense of this. But wait... I'm already standing. Then why am I only waist height when I'm really six-one? What the hell is going on? No time for answers now. I've got to run. My bones are crawling.

Panic surges up and down my spine. I turn to bolt and the doorknob greets my forehead. Damn that smarts. I slink into the hall and weave through relatives as they take the opportunity to shove their way into the room I'm trying to escape.

"Rrr... BARK!" Music to my ears. As I reach the end of the hall, my heart leaps knowing Hudson, my Miniature Fox Terrier guardian, is going to be there to greet me. I pause by the stairs and look for him in anticipation. He peels around the corner from the den and slides when he shifts from carpet to hardwood floor. Scampering to regain his footing, he pants excitedly and tears my way. But what in God's name happened to him? None of this makes any sense, but I can't sit here waiting for someone to see me... us for what we are.

Hudson runs to me and jumps to say hello. He still knows me and loves me even in this state. We turn to the stairs. I take them two at a time, hastily yet sure enough not to lose my footing. By the time I reach the top step, Hudson's already there waiting and grinning complete with tail wagging in sync.

We turn left and race down the hall. There's a mirror in the bathroom. Maybe I'm just seeing things. I grab the frame of the door as we reach it and use the momentum to swing around the corner. Bending over to catch my breath puts me at the perfect height for Hudson to reach my face with his jumping kisses.

Eyes filling with tears again, I panic at the idea of staring reality in the face. I catch Hudson mid-air and hug him with my whole heart. He uses his paws to keep my face close enough for him to reassure me and lap me repeatedly. Hudson cleans the tears streaming down my cheeks as I raise my head and look to the bathroom mirror.

My hands tremble, fighting back the inevitable. Though my body's shaking, I'm able to slide the garbage can over with my foot. Holding Hudson in one arm, I use the other to flip the can upside down and step up onto. I gaze at the mirror in shock and breathe through my gut to prevent hyperventilating.

Looking back at me in the mirror is the truth: a scared little bag of bones. Just a reflection of two skeletons where a boy and his dog should be. Hudson doesn't seem to notice the change. He's still himself despite the new appearance. He's still grinning and panting, tail still wagging. My jaw drops as I raise a hand from my side. The skeleton looking back at me does the same.

My hollow eye sockets stare through me, tears pouring out from them. My chest heaves, almost causing us to slip and fall. I step off the can, unable to look away from the mirror. Hudson squirms out from my arms and bolts around the corner to our room. I reach behind me and rest against the cabinets. Taking a final gulp still aghast, I turn and run after Hudson, slamming the bedroom door behind us.

Back pressed against the door, I slide to the floor with my head in my hands. The more I try to think this out, the less it makes sense. "Best to just sit, cry, and wait for this to pass," I tell myself. But what if it doesn't? What if we're stuck like this forever?

"Arr... row," Hudson calls from the bed. I look up to him from the floor as he grins and tilts his head, encouraging me to join him. He purrs again and lies down at the edge of the bed, staring at me. As much as I want to turn away and ignore Hudson's love, he's somehow able to melt enough of my fear to keep moving. I shake my body out and gather my bearings.

The record player sitting on my dresser catches my eye along with a dark turquoise glass pipe next to the player. My shoulders ease at the thought of checking out and listening to some records. I dart over to the opposite side of the room and flip through rows of LPs. I need to find something I can count on. My hand instinctively reaches for a record by The Smiths. I grab a jar of some buds so purple they're almost black, covered in bright and shining trichomes. "This will do the trick," I chuckle to myself.

Following some prep, I open the grinder and take a whiff of fresh purple grounds. Chills shiver through me and my fear turns to joy. I delicately pack the bowl to the brink of overflowing. I place the pipe next to the record player, grab the record I had set on the bed, and line the needle up with one of my favorite songs.

Sitting on the bed with Hudson next to me, I light a

piece of hemp wick and hold it to the corner of the bowl. The opening riff of "How Soon Is Now?" hits as I inhale a deep breath of Grand Daddy Purple. I flick a slight bit of smoke from my lips and take it back in, holding the hit until chills wash over me leaving a wake of goosebumps all over my bones. Exhaling a cloud of smoke, I feel my shoulders release their tension as my face numbs warmly and I sink into the bed.

Morrissey's voice and Marr's guitar fill the room amongst my clouds. I finish another bowl, set the pipe on the nightstand, and stretch out on the bed. Hudson stretches in full as well and crawls over to my side, settling into a stone of his own. He kisses my face and lies next to me.

A fuzzy stoned state of relaxation takes my mind away from my mother, my skeleton form, the past, present, future, and everything in between. I close my eyes and escape from myself. Escape from myself... That's it! If I could just feel like this all the time, I wouldn't care if people saw me as I am – only bones. Who am I kidding? People would run away screaming at the sight of me, but I'm onto something. I just need to find a way to be around people where I can feel numb and still blend in. So close to an idea, maybe a few more bowls will spark one.

The more I blaze, the more I feel myself change. The warm numbness spreads from head to toe, I'm finally at peace. I close my eyes and smile, baked out of my mind. Upon opening my eyes I'm greeted with the impossible. I wave my hands in front of my face. Sure enough a new set of skin, almost translucent, covers my bones. Specks of light dance in all directions between my skin and bones.

The record ends and prompts me from the bed. I turn the player off and put the record back in its sleeve. I sneak from my room to the bathroom, curious about my appearance. As soon as I crack open the bedroom door, clouds of smoke billow into the hall.

Hudson joins me as I enter the bathroom. "Unbelievable," I mutter to myself, staring at the mirror. Rather than a skeleton looking back at me, it's clear that I'm just me. The mirror's reflection looks like the regular version of me, including my regular height and weight. Though from my perspective I can tell this is just a suit shimmering with light. Scooping up Hudson, I hope the same for him, but he's still in skeleton form in both reality and reflection.

Maybe Hudson can be accepted and loved by others the way he is, but I know I've got no hope without this suit to protect me. So long as I have this plant as my fuel, I'm safe. I can stay numb and the world gets the appearance of me that's comfortable. Whatever happens going forward, I must keep them from seeing the real me. I have to keep myself from feeling the real me.

We make our way back to the bedroom to prepare. I throw on Jimmy Eat World's *Bleed American* and grab the herb grinder, a king-sized roller, papers to match, and a rolling tip. Truly a slothful stoner, I never bothered practicing how to roll and depend on the roller. As I finish prepping a joint with the last of my grounds, "Hear You Me," kicks from the speakers. I burst into tears, flashing back a couple weeks ago to them playing the same song at The Catalyst. Another flash to sharing the song with Mom and her smiling, suggesting I use it at her memorial.

My bones peek through and reveal themselves again. The stone must be wearing off since the pain and fear are coming back. I wipe my eyes, raise my chest, take a deep breath, and stand up from the bed. Hudson beside me, I raise the jay to my mouth and spark it. Waves roll over me while the song continues in the background. I set the lighter down, watch as my suit reappears with a glowing hue, and step forward.

The world around me turns to a black endless void. The walls, littered with old animation cells from films I watched as a kid, melt away like Depp's portrait from my *Fear and Loathing in Las Vegas* poster. The bed, record player, desk, dresser, it's all gone now. Everything's gone except Hudson, my cherried jay, and me. The song's chorus echoes in the background as we walk through the void.

Life plays out in time-lapse around me in all directions. Scenes play in this void at a quick pace while I hazily meander past them... Writing Mom's eulogy, guiding her casket to the front of the church with Madison, speaking in front of everyone at her funeral, waves of people coming and going at the funeral and our home afterwards.

Scenes from 2008 pass by... Dating my close friend, making out with her in the front seat of my car to *Tell All Your Friends*, lying on the Polo Fields together at Coachella, singing along together at the Colin Meloy show at the Fillmore, arguing with her more the closer we get, passive-aggressively putting her down while on vacation for not enjoying it even though I knew she wouldn't, standing her up for our anniversary dinner and sending her home early, breaking up in the process, huddling on the floor at the foot of my bed crying and smoking, staring at the clouds outside while listening to the rain and Decemberists records.

2009 memories play next... Various scenes working in retail, moving into a house with a couple coworkers, watching *Pineapple Express* and blazing with a couple other friends from work, taking Madison to his first Coachella, driving him home along the coast to San Luis Obispo and getting the idea to document this story, dating a friend from work, her picking me up on a random weeknight to surprise me with a drive to Santa Cruz and the beach, surprise trips up to Davis to visit her at school, sitting together in the front of my car with her trying to talk and help me while I blankly stare ahead.

2010... Moving into my own apartment in downtown San Jose, anxiety attacks at work, various meetings with psychologists and psychiatrists, anti-depressants turning me into a figurative zombie, a family trip to Europe, more anxiety attacks on vacation, the time capsule ceremony for my late Uncle Mike's childhood scout troop in Germany, blasting up the autobahn with cousins to Amsterdam, visiting the coffee shops, admiring the canals and architecture, checking out museums, getting home and getting a job at a cannabis collective, budtending at the shop, working in the garden while Hudson plays amongst the towering plants, suicidal audible hallucinations from the anti-depressants leading to an overdose of Ativan and rum at the apartment, waking up after a white light experience telling me I have work to do, psych ward at the hospital, Ambien tripping with a friend in the hospital and walking the halls like astronauts after everyone but the night shift had gone to sleep, an old friend visiting from New Jersey, taking her on a weekend trip to SoCal and her blurting out that she loves me, her moving in with Hudson and me, morning walks for coffee with her and Hudson, having a seizure in front of her from the anti-depressants, she and I going to a Phillies/Giants playoff game in San Francisco, her moving back to Jersey, listening to the Giants win the World Series on the radio and screaming in the front yard afterwards, Hudson and I moving out to Jersey and staying with her family, smoking out daily with her dad in the attic, sleeping on an air mattress with a hole in it on her brother's floor.

2011... Walking out of a coffee shop job in Philadelphia, walking down roads in Jersey looking for work, finding text messages on my girlfriend's phone between her and her ex about how she's still in love with him, getting a job at a computer shop in Philly, moving into a house in Philly with a friend from work, smoking with Hudson on the third floor balcony watching the city's skyline, seeing The Decemberists alone for my birthday, Thanksgiving with my girlfriend's family before breaking up.

2012... Flying out to California for Coachella, clouds everywhere for The Weeknd's set, chain-smoking joints during Dre and Snoop's set, catching The Weeknd at the TLA in Philly, 4th of July Giants/Nationals game in D.C. with longtime best friend and his fiancée, a friend from home visiting Philly, wearing Giants gear and getting on the subway full of red to see the Giants play in Philly, drinking post-win with San Francisco guys who brought a KNBR banner, dodging a fight with Phillies fans, Madison visiting Philly and us catching the Eagles and Phillies along with a jaunt up to NYC, rolling on ecstasy with coworkers and exploring an abandoned building with a lit up night view of the city, The Weeknd live at Terminal 5, Morrissey live at Radio City Music Hall, visiting an old friend from work who moved to Brooklyn, rushing to leave and make the bus back to Philly but double-backing for our first kiss and best first kiss of my life, riding the Staten Island Ferry with her and watching the New York City skyline, going to my best friend's wedding in NY with her, gloating about other hookups while at our hotel, drunkenly arguing with her and falling asleep facing opposite directions, getting off the subway and keeping eyes locked with her as the doors close and she rides away.

2013... Moving into my own row-home apartment in

South Philly with a view of the skyline, getting the call that Grandma died, flirting with a friend at work leading to hooking up after our shifts, her family asking if we're dating while at her birthday brunch, panic rising and stopping what we have, getting laid off from the Philly job, moving back to California and staying at my grandparents' empty house in San Bernardino, daily visits to Pop Pop at the rest home, seeing him scared and alone throwing tantrums when asked to eat his meals, driving up Highway 5 to job interviews in San Jose, sitting in the interviews stoned and distracting them with stories, getting a job and moving into a downtown San Jose apartment, seeing The Postal Service at the Greek with Madison, lots of drinking after work and on weekends with my boss, lots of drunk hangouts with my other best friend from high school, drunken cliché Holden-esque rants on his condo's balcony about how San Jose's changing for the worse, seeing The Weeknd at the Greek.

2014… Seeing The Hotelier in San Jose blackout drunk with my friend, talking to a girl at the bar post-show, getting up for the bathroom and returning to see my friend in my seat talking to her instead of her friend, the four of us going to his condo while he brags about his dad owning the building, falling out with him at Coachella after a weekend including him not paying his share for the camp site, inviting an extra person, and missing Pixies for PBRs back at the camp site.

Six-and-a-half years float by in rapid succession and wrap to a close as I finish the jay. Hudson continues to walk alongside me without missing a beat. The time-lapsed life events dissipate around us and fade back to a black void. I check my suit and notice it's showing signs of wear, but still intact. Whew.

When I look up, I realize we can't walk any further

ahead. A wall of various sized and style televisions stands in front of us several stories high and a city block wide. Each screen plays a different scene from the last six-and-a-half years that I had just spent trying to ignore and block out. I push against the screens in front of us. No use, they won't budge. The entire wall of televised memories bends and circles around us. Screens close in on all sides and arches overhead as well. My jay burns out, I fall to my knees, and weep. The pain of wasted time, relationships, and potential rises from my gut to a burning in my chest. I scream with all of my being and throw myself at the screens ahead, shattering them enough to break us through to the other side.

# GRIND_

CHAPTER ONE

Breathe.
BE. LOVE.

Breaking through the static...

"Be. Love." Breathe. "Be." "Love." BREATHE. "BE! LOVE!" BREATHE. Forget the distractions. "But I can't..." If you've got time to talk, you've got time to ride. And not just ride, but ride harder. These panicked breaths are proof of that. Stop with this chest nonsense and feel it in your gut. Now BREATHE. Keep riding and DON'T forget. "Be. Love. I know."

One foot clenches the pedal below while the other catches its own respectively in sync. Stop mumbling; forget the exhaust fumes of that pesky 22 Express. Sure, it's always just quick enough to leave you running for it when you've got a flat. That's the nature of buses. Just keep riding because that's yours. We take shortcuts and focus on four letters, but there's two that proceed it. Be. Let yourself in to the now because that's where you're needed. Yes. We need you. Now. More than we ever have before, which is exactly why you're here. And why you've questioned what's led you to this point the entire time. It's because you've got a perspective, ideas, passions, and dreams that need to be shared. Everyone does, somewhere inside.

Heart racing faster, our lungs pump at a rate steadier than the guitar riffs bearing down on our ear drums thanks to Joyce Manor's latest album. I hate the term 'emo,' but it's nice to see a resurgence of what made the genre great in the 80's and 90's rather than more of the same mall-punk clones that made up much of the late 00's trying to somehow grasp on to whatever last bit of the early 00's they could. Hell, even some of the greats like American Football are reuniting to bouts of adoration from longtime fans as well as new.

WHOOSH. Alright, that car came a little too close. Get home in one piece otherwise it's all for naught. The bass drum kicks in rhythm with each stride; perpetual motion. You were just thinking too much and not letting yourself ride. Breathe and take your own path home. You've taken the familiar road more times than you'd like to admit and don't need to add any more tally-marks to the record.

Riding the Alameda to or from work is typically one of the brighter parts of my day, but there's something different about this one. Can't place it, but something's off. Don't let it get to you, almost home anyways. Yeah that's true, the merge to Santa Clara Street's coming up and from there it's just a few shortcuts and back sidewalks like we used to. Sidewalks? With your bike? "It'll be quicker and the ride's nice." *Sigh.* Way to take a shortcut already. Remember how many people walk through those pathways every day? "The paths bend wide enough to fan out or weave through every-one, worst case." Exactly. Worst case, which in this case starts with taking your bike on the sidewalk. Not worth becoming part of the problem. "Plenty of people ride it too. It's just a shortcut."

Approaching the T-intersection of Stockton Avenue and West Santa Clara Street, glimpses flash across my mind. Memories from the past couple weeks in rapid succession. Too fast to focus on at first, but slowed down just right... "Oh yeah..." The construction up ahead. Don't worry about it, just take your time and keep going. A red-eyed glare from the light ahead stops us in our tracks. "Better to dodge the line altogether and ride ahead." Have it your way then. The next song kicks in as I glance down Stockton. Oncoming traffic's about to merge, but nothing out of the ordinary. Return my sights ahead to Santa Clara Street. I psych myself up, remembering I'm not much further. "Overpass. Arena. Palms. Overpass. Downtown. Shortcuts. Apartment. Hudson. Home." That's right. Get home to Hudson and get writing. Chills run down my spine. You're where you need to be. Just stay focused.

"That's weird, suddenly it got all quiet," I chuckle in victory, rocking the bike forward and back. Proudly grinning over winning an argument with myself, more weight shifts to the right leg with each push, foot at the ready. Always tell myself it's to keep my heart rate up, yet somehow each slide manages to keep rhythm with what I'm listening to at the time. Planting the balm of my left foot on the ground, I push off with the force of how little I care for waiting on that light any longer.

One thing I love about riding a bicycle is how relaxed I can feel while the rest of the world rushes by frantically. Rolling down the decline leading to the Caltrain overpass, my chuckle builds to a laugh gazing down the backed up line of cars making the turn from Stockton to Santa Clara. The wind picks up as I gain speed down the hill. Check back, ready to flash one last grin to the cars left waiting at the light. Before my lips can crack, my view catches something in the distance. Pretty dark cloud when the last week's been like a summer afternoon. Oh well, need to get home anyways. Need to see Hudson and get this down. Too much time spent collecting memories for an outlet I've spent more time talking about than using.

Eyes locked ahead, smirking widely, I glide down the hill around cars taking their time to merge. A train passes overhead, leaving from Diridon Station to somewhere up the Peninsula. Likely up to the city. Wonder if the Giants are in town? No matter for the time being, need to stay focused. Can catch them and some garlic fries next time I get.

Starting the climb up the other side, the shade from the overpass hangs longer than usual. Double-check, looking up. Not the overpass at all... Huh, didn't think rain was on the forecast, but better pick up. That cloud from the distance called up some friends who brought what look to be some deep grudges of their own. Of all the days I actually do choose to clean out that beat Alkaline Trio hoodie from the bottom of my backpack. Sighing again loudly thanks to the incline and a tinge of self-loathing, I make my way up to the next light and pause to catch my breath.

The San Jose Arena stands tall beside me to the left. Brushed steel juts down the length of each the corner spines, protecting glass windows beneath. Sunlight dances past, paying little mind to the steel's defenses and burst outward in all directions. My eye catches one beam of light in particular, brighter than the others, streak out from the window and across the length of the sweeping metal panels of the building.

What could easily be dismissed by an onlooker (or some

rival hockey fans) as a towering hunk of concrete, metal, and glass full of cold ice and hot air, this place is one of the few constants in my life. Well, except for the sign out front rented by whichever tech company shelled out this year. Kind of funny that the Arena's the perfect representation of this valley. Despite what the sign hung across the front says, people still live and play here. Year after year we keep showing up. To the games to support the team. To those companies more days than we get to spend with our families. All under the guise that there's a heart inside the machine.

Letting the years of disappointment fuel the swelling of my chest, I lean back and cross my arms, shaking my head. First at the arena. Then the people walking by, the cars whizzing past, everyone in this city including me. When did we become so proud of being proud? I watch the gleam of the building smooth and darken in shade as the clouds build heavier overhead, gaining rapidly in numbers and proximity. What do you do when the weather's as fake as these people? clap CLAPCLAPSMASH. Thunder too? Just what I need.

Panic creeps in. Deep and resonating, I feel each and every fear bubble and froth inside. Mind wanders, losing focus. Grip loosening on the handlebars, pulling myself away from not just the moment, but the bicycle as well. HONK! Whoah, of course I go and miss the light turn green.

Traffic picks up and passes on the left as I begin pedaling again, building momentum steadily. The clouds overhead darken to a sickly mix of washed out grays and blues while I feel myself give in to fatigue. "I can't," sighing defeated and winded, slowly pedaling through the intersection, passing the turn to Diridon Station. You must. Look up ahead to the Montgomery light just beyond this next stretch of construction. Keep pushing. Size up what's to come. Bright orange divider runs down the side of the right lane and looks to be close if anyone tries to pass. Chain link fencing between the divider and construction debris littering the bike lane. Wait, a gap between the divider and fence! Yeah right, not wide enough. Or just wide enough? Keep pedaling. "I just..."

HONK! HONK! "Alright!" I yell at the car behind me without bothering to look back at the driver. Pushing on and lining up with the gap ahead, I burst out laughing. Plenty of space to cruise through. Focused on the red light ahead, checking the intersection's clear, the line of cars growing beyond my plastic barrier of a shield. Forgetting something. Uh oh. Are these walls closing in or is it just me? Gut braces for impact before my foot even leans back to brake. Skidding and slowing down, the bike gives signs we'll either make the exit or have time to stop. Laugh again to myself as time slows in sync with the bike and realization that brakes are futile in this scenario.

Hugging the divider gets me past most the line of cars and just about to the light, but proves fruitless. The right handlebar catches one of the gaps in the chain link for a moment, throwing the front wheel into a slight veer and wobble. Brace the handlebars firmly with both hands, steadying the bike's aim as straight ahead as possible despite the closing surroundings. Determined, I grit my teeth and keep pedaling. Left shoe brushes plastic, I pull in tighter. Right shoe grazes fencing. Not much left I can do at this point, but give it one more solid push. Plastic wears against my left knee, surely leaving some of me with it. The pain stings, but I know it's just a sign of the impact about to come. As I reach the end of the construction, the path finally proves too narrow for my bicycle, causing the handlebars to catch each respective wall and send me careening over the handlebars.

I pass the freshly green-lit streetlight ahead of traffic, wearing a grin that I know will only last this moment while midair before the concrete greets me with the results of my own actions. Already at peace before I hit the ground, I'm able to breathe deeply and gain control long enough to tuck a shoulder and roll roughly, but safely to a stop out of the way of traffic. I get through the light first because of getting thrown off only to stand up and collect the bike along with myself as lines of cars pass.

Assessing the situation, I notice that my knee got the worst of the scuffs and scrapes. Nature was kinder than I was to myself. If I had just been patient instead of pushing ahead... So tired of always being the cause of my own end before actually starting anything. No time for self-loathing now. That decaying feeling in your gut isn't just internal. Looking up again the clouds bear down worse than before. No sign of sky beyond, just swarming black clouds filling out at a steadier pace than I had been keeping on bike.

Before I come to, I find myself somehow pedaling down Santa Clara Street. The bicycle, though wobbling in line with its rider, remains steady and vigilant in its path. Guided by palm trees on both sides of the street a flash of light catches my eye in the reflection of the bike's logo. Focusing my double vision, the loose resemblance of reds, blues, yellows, and grays focus their hues to remind me of my bike's name painted on the side of the frame: Hudson Hornet. *FLASH* **HUDSON!**

My sight strays from the path ahead and further into the concrete below me. Watching the path by looking down only lets me see the steps next to and behind. Heart and gut anchor the body and jolt the mind. Another *FLASH* BARK! **HUDSON!**

The soul has a stronger memory than my mind ever could. The body is keeping this bicycle on its path home to love. As the gut and heart work in tandem to shock the mind and in turn the rest of my body, I can feel again. Love again. Hudson's not just at home, he's here now. In my heart with love cheering me to get up in this moment. In each moment. To keep stepping forward in light and love for me. For us. For all.

Blinking a few times, I shake my head and redirect my vision upwards. Hits me that while fear kept me from looking ahead and seeing light, there was always time.

The ride down Santa Clara Street from that point's as blurry as I chose to let myself become when Hudson's love was staring me in the face the entire time. While the ride may have been long, short, an eternity, or just a day, life, or passing moment, I wasn't to judge.

Climbing to the door from the strewn bicycle abandoned in the driveway, I've let myself detach this time without even paying for a doctor's excuse or another bottle of anti-depressants. What the hell did I let myself do? Nothing. Exactly. I just let my heart and instinct share horror stories at their pity party while my ego chooses to drown in bottle after bottle. Dragging myself along the pavement and through each miserable memory. Missing Pixies for PBR'S? Check. Flushing my eighteenth birthday's check and dignity down my jeans? Check. Every regretful morning. Every regretful choice. Hazy or otherwise. They are the same: based in fear.

Fear slows my journey to the light ahead with every moment I refuse to let go and look forward. Barking again. Looking ahead I focus. Just pavement. Can't even bear to raise my head. The strength leaves my fingertips that had been gritted, pulling me forward to the apartment door. I lie down and cry. Huddled on the ground. Bike somewhere outside my peripheral on the driveway. Tears flow. Another flashback. Great. Thinking about almost losing Hudson while riding home with him and my demons steering the handlebars. All the while grinning and happily mistaking each weave's warning as my own prideful design. I still don't know how we made it home that night, but I was grateful.

Gratitude brings me to the present. Blinking again we look around and listen. No one. Just me. Whew. What a relief no one saw this mess of a person crumpled on his own patio. Gathering the bike from the driveway along with what's left of my self-esteem, I turn the corner.

A light glows from the room that I had never seen.

Though the windows are cloudy and my vision hazy

I let go and

am

peace.

Eyes ahead now instead of at the ground, there is a light from within that raises me and brings me home. This and every time. Somehow we come home. A steady pulse of light coursing from the room and welcoming clouds escape from the crack under the door I had locked.

Letting go, my body knows how to come home. We all do.

We let go and listen to each moment.

This one opens the door.

CHAPTER TWO_


10/9/14

I'm at the chicken place after work grabbing some beers and food with my boss and another coworker.

My coworker's talking about taking his family to the beach and taking his son through the water. Was a point where he went under on his own, got scared, reached his arm up and his dad was there. Later said "the water scared me," ... "but I was there wasn't I?" ... "yup." ... Clicks with me. Keep feeling like I drowned in a past life, but am so connected to the water in this one. This split has fascinated me my whole life. How at home yet petrified I've felt at the same time while I've been treading. Much like life I'm finding. This is all for a reason. This life I face my fears. This is where I break through. This is where I rise up out of the water and get up on the board instead of letting my self-imagined squid pull me under.

It's fucking ten o'clock seven years after I watched my own mother die in front of me and I still have the fucking gall to give in to what others think about me and my work. I'm so fucking tired of bending over backwards for systems and lemmings of such that just don't fucking give a shit. I blew a whole night and the cost of some records on a night trying to level with my boss only to find that work hasn't had my back from day one. This place is just like the rest. I can only help these people when I'm alone. They not only refuse to understand me, but refuse to understand while I'm helping, before and after. The fact that walking in between service calls with headphones on is a sin yet getting drunk with my boss is fine.

Some stream of consciousness aside, guess what?

I'm mad at myself enough for giving in and paying more to drink with people that don't respect my views, opinions, efforts, and beliefs. I won't let them stop me from documenting it. I'm mad at myself for walking into that last bar tonight. My boss's words still sting and ring in my ears from when I showed reluctance at the bar's front door and asked, "Are you looking for a friend or enabler?" He replied chuckling, "The latter."

Even when I've turned the night around into a productive night blazing with Hudson, listening to Cake records, and writing my heart out, I find ways to self-criticize. It's because we're always growing and learning. We need to improve and get better. Evolve or die. I just want us to in the write vein.

I'm still too scattered, still too drunk. My boss's friend called me out tonight and it resonated. I had him like I have most until I cave. It's like the Sharks' playoffs of words. I don't care much about any of them and I hate that this is so circular this keyboards a damn punching bag it keeps going just give me something back i hate just being me and this and ust and this god damn screen fucking do something already. I hate being in the moment and feeling absolutely nothing. It feels fucking empty like i do every morning when i wake up only to give what's left to people who don't appreciate it and not only that crave more than you even know how to give.

You need and deserve a positive distraction because you're driving yourself crazy driving yourself for others. Drive yourself for you and you'll finally find a road worth traveling. Fuck all this other nonsense. Once you forge a path that's clear and safe the rest will follow. Stop insulting them for not knowing better. Breathe. Live in the moment. Even the most earnest like my boss are like Icarus. We are human.

I. am. human.

This. Is. It.

Was just about to get up, put on a tv show, but felt it pull again. I can't put this keyboard down as much as I try it's a part of me. Grabbed the laptop and then "Let Me Go" came on. It's poetry in motion. Life imitating art imitating art. It's hearing new-found beauty in my favorite songs. It's about rediscovering love when I thought I spent my entire life fighting for it just to let it slip away.

She's looking just as hard I am and we're getting closer. Ignore all distractions. Ignore all people. It's just you and me now until we make this. Leave work at work. Leave this here so that we can make it. This is happening.

Only eight more hours left. to go.

Finally a change from what I've been looking at all day. I'm so tired of watching my friends, colleagues and heroes give in to the machine. Enjoy your day as a battery, folks. Not for me.

It's all for me which is why I'm here. I need to take a vow of silence and just write for a month to see how I feel.

And it begins.

And resonates. Even after pausing and setting the

computer down for a bit. Coming back to the laptop after putting on the Prawn split and starting it from the front for the first time rather than cheating and starting from Side B. Already something's different. Whether it holds, we'll see, but I at least initially want to live more honestly. Not just with words, but with action.

I've nailed words, but my actions have yet to follow. Perhaps this is where I learn to catch up to my mouth? Why else take a vow of silence in 2014 at 28? Even sitting here alone on my bed, back against the wall, polished pint of ice cream beside me, I find myself trying to scream, but only having a keyboard in front of me. I must learn to let these words carry their weight and let them ebb and flow with the tide rather than trying to fling each off the coast. This won't be easy. People will understand me less. Those who already do will still get me. Both are why I'm here. We're all worth it. This all is. Which is why we're here and there's still time. It doesn't matter the scenario, environment, or distractions because you're there for a reason.

Stay tuned in.

Tune in yourself.

Time to flip the 7". Yay, now Prawn.

Sitting back down. I flash back to seventh grade dances and basketball games in the yard. Despite how scared I convince myself I am to move forward alone, I realize that's how I've always done it before. Even back then, I was the one to navigate different social groups, talk to girls, yet always get heckled by my main group of friends. They were the cowards, but I couldn't deal with that or them. We're in this together even if they won't understand. If Dad can understand this soon with what we've been through, then this is all worth it. Keep going. Don't say a word tomorrow. Now get some rest.

Mom. I love you. And miss you.

I almost tried to go to bed without being honest about why this started. Or is this why it started? We'll see, but this is part. I talk too much. Tonight, it let me spend too much to drink too much to say too much to lose too much. I'm tired of losing before I've started something so much better than what I've worked for before. Need to keep going. Get a small notepad and pen tomorrow. Don't take a drink tomorrow or ever again. Just take it a day at a time.

CHAPTER THREE

Day 2 - Sat. 10/11/14

It's Saturday morning. This is important which is why the dark didn't want me to document Day One. This process heals. I need to learn to love not just the process, but my process. I believed until now that that may be selfish. What is selfish is hiding my gifts within the cell I've built for myself.

Throughout the day yesterday, I was in a surface meditative state. I panicked less. I listened more. I put thought into what I was about to say, not into the continuous effort to keep talking. I care more about others for their reasons, not my own. I feel their pains, joys, and every subtle emotion inferred consciously or subconsciously along the way.

Recap the events of the day. There is much to be learned even when reflecting back. The trick is not to dwell and lose yourself to the emotions, but rather be silent and listen to them just as I listened to those outside myself.

I love *Evil Dead 2* and those types of films because they're real life. Life is hell. Life is the horror story. I want to be like Ash. I want to be the comic relief, but a constant at the same time. By giving himself to the moment and those around him with his unique gifts, he was able to prevail and inspire generations of people who thought they were untouched and unloved. I want every single living being on this earth to know we are one.

Life is hell. Life is what we make. What if Earth was hell? Immediate reaction is repelling. I've learned that that feeling is the one we need to shine the light on rather than run. I'm exhausted from running away from my own fears. What if we each individually chose to turn from that love? This becomes an opportunity rather than a damning then. The fact that there is this much beauty in hell means that we don't have to live like this. We're already dead because we chose to walk away from that love.

This life is longer than we allow ourselves to believe it is.

We can walk back. We can run. We can build contraptions and whizzbangs and dream machines to get us there even faster. The brighter we make hell, the sooner it becomes heaven.

I've believed I was here because I wasn't loved. How selfish.

This work is far from over, but the darkest days are over because I finally believe they are. Nature presents obstacles, yet however large they may seem, we are capable of learning how to overcome them and use them to make us stronger. The obstacles we set for ourselves are the ones we'll never overcome unless we chose to do so. Each and every single day.

Took a break from writing.

Breaks with purpose still have that. Distractions are not breaks.

Took a good tangent with Ash, but still need to go through yesterday before I can focus on today.

Fascinating. Even reflecting, I remember faces and people instead of times and things I was doing. So look at the day in terms of that. Hands are already tired. Reminder of how tired I felt at the end of yesterday. Need to rethink. Need to type less.

Even after moving to the next paragraph, the first emotion is guilt. Why? Following. I've left out people. Whether in passing and looking away after eye contact or not going out of my way to seek out more people, I focus on how I'm not doing enough.

Without darkness there are only those that I've helped and those I'm going to help. Yesterday I encountered a good amount of people and my silence was overwhelmingly positive, for myself and them. The only times that faltered were because of my approach and those I felt most guilty about.

This quiet is teaching me to quiet my inner voices as well. My own devices become distractions and devastate. I am but a vessel and need to listen to that higher love in every moment instead of tuning in at my convenience. My convenience doesn't have the same wisdom and ever-present, forgiving love. The love that welcomes at each moment, inviting us to take part as well.

Records bring me peace. Even when artists sing of hate and negativity, they love themselves and others enough to share their struggle in hopes of helping others get through theirs. It's time we share this story. Our story.

Instead of rambling and letting ideas run away from themselves, I need to reflect and focus on each moment and word to best deliver their cause and message. It isn't my message. It is the message of love and that is universal. When I speak I infuse my ego with the message. While a perspective is important, a bias is the dark seeping into the light. Be strong enough to listen. Be courageous enough to do instead of say.

Focus on the positive and document the progress.

Met up with a priest that afternoon and was honest with him about my drinking. As much as I persist with the notion that I can't get through this struggle alone, what if I look at that in a positive light? See it as an opportunity to grow and ask for help. It starts by taking the first step and writing down that I have a problem. I choose where the foot gets placed going forward now. I choose not to slide. I choose to pick up and carry on. That priest provided more guidance than I could have asked or hoped for. I need to stop and just be. That's when the beauty unfolds around me.

CHAPTER FOUR

10/11/14 - Saturday evening

Just as I was about to give in and start scrolling back through today's journal entry, I could finally hear Pop Pop. Usually it's Mom and Grandma, sometimes Uncle Mike. This time it was Pop Pop clear as day. I miss him so much.

Those couple weeks with him were some of the best of my life. As difficult as our time was together, it was spent together completely and that's what matters. I look up to him so much and what he's done for his family.

I am no longer trying to be half the man he is. I am trying to be me. The man he couldn't be which is why he started his family and sacrificed all he could. He did it so he wouldn't have to hide anymore. We won't hide anymore. I love you so much Pop Pop. I have a drinking problem and Pop Pop is cheering me on towards getting better. At first I was overwhelmed that he reached out. Now I'm at peace.

Took a long walk with Hudson today. We went through SJSU, back down 4th St. to Reed, almost went over to The Plaza de César Chávez, but Hudson looped a block twice instead. Got frustrated, but remembered to breathe and go with nature. Inspiration comes through repetition. TV On The Radio over my earbuds helps keep me at peace. I was just tired, but kept going for him. We made it to the park near the apartment and pursued a few more blocks.

Wanted to write, but didn't feel like anything was there. Took a shower, threw on *Home, Like Noplace Is There* and ate a pb/banana sandwich. Sat with the laptop for a bit before setting it down, knowing I can't force it. I'm at peace and where I need to be. Just keep searching for Solace Valley.

CHAPTER FIVE

Day 3 - Sun 10/12/14

The dark still tries to creep in. It's 7:16pm, bottom of the 6th in Game 2 of the NLCS in St. Louis. Giants tied up 2-2. Taking it play by play. Just like I'm learning to take liking life rather than just the result. I've been tired both physically and mentally, but there is a fire that burns brighter than ever before.

Ever since we locked eyes last night, everything's changed.

Keep writing, even when you're tired. That's when you need to push harder to get your message out. That's when your message is most important. Tired is a distraction.

Back on track.

Saturday was some kind of magic. Did a fairly good job of taking notes during the day, but from the start it felt almost like a dream state. The only times it didn't was when I was scared of what I was being set up for. Now that I know she exists, there is no fear. Now I know her eyes. Now I know her smile, her laugh. Beauty in its purest form. All around us.

There was a sense of wonder in that room last night. I'll never forget how quickly all the lighters in the room went up, including hers. I had my vape pen. The fear dissipates immediately as we brush arms, and meet eyes again, then scan the room together taking in this moment. Our moment. "Fucking amazing..." she says. I can't think of any better description.

The dark tried to keep me away from the show. I almost gave in to going to the Sharks game instead, scared I'd let down those offering the tickets. Felt relief knowing I'd rather go see The Weeknd up in SF.

Almost let the dark take me again and miss the train. Lingering in my cell, the sick feeling in the pit of my stomach isn't as acidic as it used to be. I stamp it down, knowing I'll get there despite running behind. I haven't missed the train until I watch it leave the station without me on it.

Made the train with a minute and a half to spare. That was the most important 90 seconds of my life.

I took several notes that night, but one line especially rings true which I will never let myself forget: "I can't remember the last time I didn't ride the Caltrain drunk. I can't remember the last time I enjoyed a ride on the Caltrain." Until now. This train was traveling to San Francisco, but in turn brought me home both trips.

Along the ride, I found that my regular dispensary closed earlier than I expected and would be closed by the time I arrived. Panic and the dark set in and held longer than I wanted, but was still manageable. I channeled. Lined up a couple options, the lesser looking one on the way to the safe bet.

The first club I stopped by didn't know how to approach customers with disabilities. Upon looking around, they didn't know how to approach customers. The gentleman checking me in looked sad and apologized a lot, but refused to help or listen. Tried slowing down and adapting my approach, but I must accept when others refuse my help.

The defeated sigh I let out grounded me to the times where I did the same towards someone who couldn't communicate in the way I was pushing. If we are able to bend and help someone who cannot, there is no choice: we must. That is why we have the capability, not to push ourselves further at their cost. While I was proud for not speaking, I was disappointed in negatively reacting. There is fear in reacting. We are all constants and need to be confident enough to embrace the responsibilities of such a calling. We need to be humble enough to listen and not give in to the distractions of our own voice and inner voice.

Following the sigh, I reset and left. Before doing so, I looked back and tried to motion that I wouldn't come back. Not only is that still reactionary and the opposite of what I am, they clearly had no idea what I meant since I was just making random hand motions to them.

In my gut, I knew that shop was going to be a bad experience before I went in but still did so anyways. This was one of the last times I make a decision like that. The hike to an old favorite spot cemented this with each step.

Upon arriving I was hoping for a good experience, but was actively preparing for a repeat of the last place. Erase that fear as soon as I met the gentleman at the front of the collective. He radiated love and happiness. As soon as he read my note about my silence, his face somehow got even happier. He shared his experience of a 10 day vow of silence and the immeasurable impact it's held for him. We said more between eye contact than body language or speaking could. He could see my realization of this in that moment and promptly bowed as I quickly followed. The gentleman at the counter, while not as in sync as I and the former, tried harder than most anyone yet I've encountered to adapt his communication style. Watching him do so fueled my own adaptation to his style. Before we knew it we were on the same page. All love takes is us saying YES.

Love is that simple. That's what so beautiful about it.

I left that place not just in a better mood than I went in, but the best mood I had been in yet that day. This is all for a reason. Feeling everything lining up.

Get to city hall and pause, admiring the orange glow basking the building. Make it into the Bill Graham Civic, take a look at the merch and quickly move on. Feeling pulled more than ever. I somehow walk to the exact spot I need to be in. Plenty of drunks bumping into each other and myself. This no longer gets to me as much and reinforces what I am doing.

We catch eyes. That's all it takes for everything to change.

I continue to struggle with finding peace in my uncomfortableness. But now. Now when I try to struggle, all I find is peace. Instead of seeking conflict, I only want to be near her and I don't know why.

The crowd shifts through Schoolboy Q's opening set. He's embracing this moment. I worry less about those bumping into me and more about how far I'm bumped away from her. Each time we meet eyes it's like the first time. Each time she brushes my arm with hers it's like I'm being touched for the first time.

Life moves slowest when we're in the moment so that we can listen and take part in it.

In between sets I start to load my pen with some wax.

I've gotten good at noticing when I'm being watched. As I'm about to load a glob of GSC, the guy in front of me slings his jacket off, only bumping me enough to lose the dab. I'm well aware of her reaction because it's my counterpart's reaction. I'd react the same way. In this moment, I don't audibly sigh, but go animated face instead and silently laugh about it. The moment's tapping me on the shoulder.

I look over and confirm. She's real. This is happening and she's reacting just as I would. I smile widely, already feeling something in my heart I haven't felt in this life yet.

Reload the pen. There will always be bud, no need to worry. I am fully at peace in this moment. As soon as I finish loading and settle in for Abel to take the stage, I catch myself giving her an equally animated look as before. Why? Because she's pulled out the fattest blunt I've seen rolled. The moment's knocking me upside the head.

The show starts. We begin to get in our zone. I realize she is lone like me. Not only that, but houses the majority of the blunt before sharing with a guy next to her who I hadn't seen before. As they finish, I try to give myself reasons why this isn't happening. The audible beating out of my chest shuts my head up pretty quickly. More so with each subsequently shorter gasp from my inner-dark.

Something's different with the dark. It doesn't have the same weight. I notice the muscle memory of those voices creeping in, but that's all they are. Memories. The dark will try, but not within me anymore. Took a minute to let the last sentence sink in.

I count on bringing myself down, but now it's not just me. It's us. There was never any dark. There is only light. The brightest, warmest, most loving light.

We are in the moment of our own show and together at the same time. We keep drifting towards each other and brush like magnets. As soon as one finds the other, we're home. The lighters and taking in the room together felt as if they were all cheering for us finding each other.

She has the most beautiful smile.

Especially loved her stoned grin - it melted me. When I noticed the guy she had shared the blunt with had left and wasn't there with her to begin with, I offered the pen. She just looked up grinning politely. We never had to say anything because she knew everything about me just by looking at me. She saw me.

If it was possible to fall in love several times in one time, this night was it.

As the show closes and the song is ending, I get flashbacks and the feeling of déjà vu.

I feel her leaving before I watch her go.

I don't even have to walk over to her, I float. Tap her shoulder and point over to the side so we can stop. I don't even have to explain, she knows.

I type frantically, "Really funny timing since I just took a vow of silence. You are the most breathtaking person I have met and would do just about anything to get to know you. Hi. I'm Morgan. :)"

Hand her the phone, watching her eyes the entire time. I'm already fighting back tears when she looks up with the same exact look. She types away on my phone and hands it back to me.

Her phone number. And her name. Leslie.

CHAPTER SIX_

Day 4 - Mon 10/13/14

When God calls, it is imperative to answer. As difficult as it may be for that time and place, that is likely the very reason we're called by name and blessed with individually unique gifts and perspectives. When we let our mind and emotions be our tools instead of our steering wheel, we can truly listen and be open for what is truly needed from us.

The world needs love. The world needs more people with flashlights. Spotlights. Stadium lights. We need to burn as bright as the sun. Only then can we move forward together.

I've been singing lyrics to myself since my time spent with Pop Pop. I've let the dark allow me to only believe writing meant one form. Love is boundless. If we can, we must. As I continued to write, I let myself believe I couldn't be musically creative and pigeonholed myself to the journals and story in progress. Then I listened to my friend's demos.

Everything changed.

Again.

In less than two days.

As I listened to his songs with him, I knew then but didn't know how to process it. Raced home, spent quality time with Hudson at the park, and met the most peaceful couple I've seen in this city since I was a kid. Looped back to the house and gave in to anxious pacing. Caught myself, using that as a clue rather than trigger.

Without fear, each opportunity is clear as day.

His music inspires. The South Bay has a sound and this is it.

Put on the computer's visualizer and settled in for the first listen. Let the songs wash over me and understand what it's like to live in this oxymoron of a city. He understands and has the most hopeful undercurrent throughout each song. He feels their pain because it's his pain. A pain and fear that's carried on generations. It's time for our generation to accept and fight for love. We are capable of writing a new chapter. The next chapter, not the one promised down the road by the introduction countless pages and lives behind.

People are not batteries. They are instruments of love here for a reason.

We need to show them that. Telling them hasn't worked. They live through screens. Not each other. We need to stand on top of their skyscrapers, scream it as loud as we can and trust that enough will come with us that we can start anew.

As I let the album resonate with me, I feel peace. I feel hope. I know this is the time. The time for love to win. Because that is all there is. Fear is a filter created by man. We did not create ourselves. We need to trust our higher calling and use our fear as a tool. Keep it stored in our gut, let it remain just as slight indigestion, only calling on it when focused into some form of creative outlet. We are creators, not followers. Not just a few, but all. Each. And every. We need to stand up and not just act like it. But do. We need to create because that is the only scenario we have not tried yet as man.

History repeats itself unless we believe it does not have to. Unless we abandon the inherent fear instilled in each of us by our self-created environment. Love is real. Love is magic. Life is magic. That is not something to be taken lightly. Or feared. It is to be embraced, seized, honed, refined, and then fired off into the sky like it is the last flare and only flare we were ever meant to bear. If not now, then when? We keep repeating because we choose to. We need to choose love. Be. Love.

As I went through my second listen, I grabbed my phone and started punching away notes. What the song made me feel, what I saw. I made it to the start of track 3 and the phone's screen flickered and went out. Watching the old version of me give in to fear and take it as a sign 'no' only lasted a brief instant. I laugh at fear now. It is like a hammer throwing a temper tantrum that I had to use a screwdriver. I know why fear tried at that moment. Which is why I kept going.

Track 1 - The song I have always wanted for the drive through the Santa Cruz hills. Climbing the hill we have done so many times. When I see the trees, I feel. The wind flows from them to us. Fueling our journey to Solace Valley.

Track 2 - Towers, dust, East hills, ants, batteries, hope, rebuild

Track 3 - Grandma and Pop Pop's empty house while I walked the halls. Our cross is only generational if we choose to pick it up.

Track 4 - What better end than a car crash?

CHAPTER SEVEN_

10/13/14

There is no more lucid dreaming. Lucid dreaming is living.

These tears are the opposite, the complete other end of the spectrum from those I've shed for the last seven years. The last twenty-eight years. The last countless lives it's been since I've seen her smile and love from within her eyes. She knows me. All of me. And loves every part of me. I don't have to say anything. She knows I feel the exact same way. All we can do is shed tears together and smile.

CHAPTER EIGHT

Day 5 - Tues 10/14/14

Get home and put on *Between Bodies* by The World Is A Beautiful Place & I Am No Longer Afraid To Die. Don't write at first, just take in the record.

Flip to Side B.

Stay in the moment. Breathe, close my eyes, silence. Complete. Listen. I can see now.

I remember. I remember everything.

The floods rush back. High seas. We are brothers in arms. He is my best friend from years ago. Lives ago. He is my first mate. It is all coming back with each wave over the bow, dragging the ship further under. I sealed our fate. We both sealed ours leaving our families ashore. Our soulmates waved goodbye and we collectively knew it was the last.

Until now.

Record ends.

I can't believe we got another chance. We get another chance. Each moment is that chance. Now is that moment.

I always believed, but lived in fear. Fear covers memories, distorts reality. Reality is what you make. They're already ghosts walking. Heads down. Screens bright. Not ants. Ants march together. They walk alone.

I remember those long drives down the 5. They felt like a lifetime. Sitting on the backseat with my brother watching VHS tapes on that small tv. Our parents put up with so much. We all smile together as we arrive. The journey is long. The journey hard. Some will fall. Others will take their own paths. Some will stray. We have to light the torch. Restore the hope. Give light to the dark. Love is all. And ever will be. Remove the filter. Love is all there is.

Love is an open door. Accepting friends as family. Breaking bread, sharing time. Presents under the tree. Stockings stuffed. Toddlers to teens to adults. Sons to fathers to grandfathers. We don't walk alone. We walk together. For each other. For who's next. For what's to come. Together. We can choose love. There's still time.

But then days turn toweekstomonthstogoddamnyears I've lost track now. I've lost my

Mind. Is just a tool in the drawer. In my grandfather's drawer. It's empty now. So's the fridge. Where are they? Where am I? What happened? They were just here a minute ago weren't they? Grandma? Pop Pop? Mom? Dad? Madison? Where are you? I need you.

Loop the end twice.

I'm sick. And tired. And this heaving in my gut won't go away. I've been here before. Countless times. These rooms used to be filled with people and memories of better times, but that's all that's left. Me and these empty rooms. These hallways. That lead to just another cell I've built for myself. No matter how many times I retrace my steps, I can't find them. But I won't forget.

Kept going with writing to the music. Wrote one good song and great starts to two others. For my first time attempting to write lyrics. Be present in each moment and abandon fear.

Found myself looping and editing. Good to be aware, but need to save a separate draft as soon as I'm out of my lucid writing state. Then edit a duplicate if need be. Editing is a tool which can be useful, but not when running the show. Got up and took Hudson out front. When walking back, we walked next to a car, but a drunk had to lean against it the entire way, forcing us to move for him. "Sorry," he mumbled, looking at the ground.

I needed both of those reminders that I am still human. Stay humble and present. These are not my words, but rather our words. Be selfless with them, not selfish and controlling. Let them flow, never overthink them. Be. Love.

Got up this morning, still dark outside. Was diligent in not letting my dark prevent me from setting an alarm last night. Phone was on the fritz, so I adapted. Love adapts. Love is always present. Love knows no bounds. Tested the alarm on the laptop to find no sound. Set up a couple alarms to be safe. 5:00am it is. Start off with your workout.

Check the clock. 6:24. What feeling do I have? Love. Peace. Was expecting fear to cripple me and make me late from the panic of missing the gym. Instead, I see opportunities. I needed the rest. The right thing happened at the right time because it did.

Found the phone working again. Bizarro.

Oh well, means I get to listen to the ep on the ride now. Damn. Life is so funny. I used to fear my destiny. Now I embrace it. Love is all there ever was and ever will be. We need to share this message. We need to scream it with every last ounce of our being. Only then can we inspire others to shine their lights just as and even brighter. And only then can we finally erase dark and fear completely from this world.

Each track made sense for each part of the ride and connected even deeper to the themes speaking to me through the music last night. Track 1 during the getting up and go part of the ride, through SJSU, on the way to Santa Clara St. Track 2 down Santa Clara St. with the heavy guitar hitting right next to the newest skyscraper started since I moved back. The hopeful part from the bridge hits right as I'm getting to the overpass and row of palm trees. A single palm tree rises as the ants build their towers to compete. When the towers fall, palms will be all that's left.

Track 3 as I'm passing by the arena. I've seen this all before. Generations. My father walking me to my first Sharks game. His dad taking him places and trying to inspire. What have we done as a generation with the level that's been set? It's time to drop fear and love each other as people. Look past any obstacles and just see another being. We are all connected. That's not something to fear, that's something to be excited about. We're all in this together. Tears of sorrow, missing my grandparents at the start of the song turn to tears of joy by the end, passing rows of new condos, knowing I refuse to be a battery.

Track 4. It's time for action. I'm getting close to work. What happens when we hit that wall? Do we let ourselves burn in the wreckage or do we dig every ounce of strength to climb out of our fear and turn the wheel before we hit the wall? Headlines go as I look out the window at a new generation practicing on the field. I don't see ants anymore, I see love and hope.

10/14/14 8:44 PM

Track 1

Chorus

Heading down this road we've taken so many times before.

Must we climb them once again each time pushing more?

We don't see the walls ahead, just keep winding paths.

To distract ourselves we drive expensively and fast.

Morgan Spoken Word

Climbing the hill. These roads wind. They hug the hills. They embrace me. They embrace us. Not just the roads, but the hills themselves. They were always alive. And so are we. It's time to wake up. Remember? These trees have memories. The wind blows through from them to us. It blows through all of us. Let the wind carry us. Let our souls heed their calling. Let our bodies be gracious enough to trust enough to listen in silent solidarity. There is strength in silence. There is strength in love. So STAND UP AND BE. LOVE.

Chorus

Morgan SW 2

We're just as part of nature as the constant flowing stream. If we push just a little bit further, we'll reach our destiny. Listen to yours. Seize your courage as nature does. Be the river ever flowing, constant. Not just the leaf following currents, only to get blocked by the simplest of rocks. Be the tree. Be constant. Shed your leaves. Shed your fears. Remove the stones we set in front of ourselves, between each other. We are the obstacles. No one else. It is on us to let our rivers overflow with love. Clear your river of debris and join nature. Join each other. BE. LOVE.

Track 2

Clouds gather in the East. We meet the horizon's gaze. Swirling darkly overhead.

Dust circles around us. Clouds the horizon. Clouds our hearts. Fear turns us to dust. We're dust. Nothing but dust.

We are at the gates. We are towers. And screens. And dust. Remove the filter. Abandon your fear. Incinerate your screens. Set fire to your hearts. All that is left is love. All we are is love. Abandon fear. We are love. We are not fear. So do not be afraid. BE. LOVE.

We build our own hourglass and fill it with our souls. Our hopes our dreamslovesneighborsfriendsfamilies Ourselves. Until there's nothing. Nothing left but dust.

And clouds. Darker. Stronger. They do not follow me. They carry me. These clouds will give way to light. Light we bring. Light we restore. This is our time. Not yesterday. Today. Right. NOW.

We are brothers in arms. We build together. Fight together. Die together.

Nothing but dust. All these towers. Just cells. Ants building more cells on top of cells on top of cells coffins and coffins it is not a condo it is a morgue they are not ants they are agents of death we all are every time we build another brick another stone cast against each other instead of these walls we are building between us. These screens. Nothing but distractions. Living through distractions for distractions. Every time you buy in. Every time you buy something. Anything. Everything. It is just paper. It is just a label. We are just labels. And paper. And dust. I am sick. This acid in my gut just scrapes me away. Away from us. Away from love. Away from where we are meant to go. Meant to be.

I refuse to buy in. I refuse to drink your poison. Those bottles are just distractions like all the screens these ghosts live through. Erasing our memories one sip at a time. Fear erases our memories. Our souls. Our love. Ourselves. I will take your poison and use it as the fuel to burn the rest of your towers down so we can start anew. We will take the shattered remains, make them our friends, show them love, and begin again.

So what if your dad owns a building? Does he own your soul? How much did you sell it for? Was it worth it? What are YOU WORTH? Watch that paper burn to dust along with YOU and the TOWERS. And the SCREENS. And ME. And US.

Unless.

There is still time. To BE. LOVE.

Track 3

Instrumental chorus

SW: I remember those long drives down the 5. They felt like a lifetime. Sitting in the backseat with my brother watching Disney VHS tapes on that small tv. Our parents put up with so much..Oh we just can't wait to be kings. We already are. We all smile together as we arrive. The journey is long. The journey is hard. Some will fall. Others will take different paths. Some will stray. We have to light the torch. Restore the hope. Give light to the dark. Love is all. And ever will be. Remove the filter. Abandon fear. Love is all there is. SO STAND UP AND BE IT. BE COUNTED. AS A PERSON. NOT. A. NUMBER. BE. YOU. BE. LOVE.

Love is an open door. Accepting friends as family. Breaking bread, sharing time. Sharing ourselves. Presents under the tree. Toddlers to teens to adults. Sons to fathers to grandfathers. We don't walk alone. We walk together. For each other. For who's next. For what's to come. Together. We can choose love. There's still time.

Instrumental chorus

But then days turn toweekstomonthstogoddamnyears I've lost track now. I've lost my

Mind. Is just a tool in the drawer. In my grandfather's drawer. It's empty now. So's the fridge. Where are they? Where am i? What happened? They were just here a minute ago weren't they? Grandma? I can't hear your laugh. Pop Pop? I can't smell your pancakes. Mom? I can only hug your memories now. Dad? When did you grow so tired? Madison? Where did you hide that spark? Where are you? I need you. Each and every one of you. I need you more than ever to choose love. Turn away from fear and know that love is always waiting for your return with an open door and open arms. So STAND UP AND BE IT. BE. LOVE.

Instrumental chorus

Scream: I'm sick. I'm tired. And this heaving in my gut won't go away.

Repeat

Repeat

Down all these empty hallways. To all these empty rooms. I search for feelings I know died with them. I know. I. died. with. them.

Repeat

Repeat

SW: I've been here before. Countless times. These rooms used to be filled with people and memories of better times, but that's all that's left. Me and these empty rooms. These hallways. That lead to just another cell I've built for myself. No matter how many times I retrace my steps, I can't find them. But I won't forget. So stand up. BE. LOVE.

10/14/14 - MIDDLE OF THE NIGHT.

Woke up. About to fall asleep again.

Muzzle in the mail slot. Brandy sniffing madly to greet while Midnight jumps alongside. I feel them visit me. Chasing each other around the room and hopping onto the bed and me. Then the rest of the family dogs that have died follow suit and dog pile me alive as ever. Minnie and Mickey. Nikita. Shasta. Mom's Irish Setter. Dad's poodle. They all start to play, but Minnie and Mickey trot up together and start tag team attacking my face with kisses before I could retrieve my hands from under the covers to stop them. Immediately felt peace dissolve my sorrow and fear and just let myself be present to so many old friends caring enough to visit all at once. I'm on the right path and they're cheering me on. Each step towards love and light is a step closer to them. I used to be petrified of that idea. Now it fills me with tears of joy knowing that they're not only waiting, but bursting at the seams with longing and missing just as I have since we parted ways on this plane in these forms.

Was about to go to sleep again, thinking that was it. Thinking too much. It's just beginning.

CHAPTER NINE

10/15/14 5:59 AM

Pray. Pray hard in gratitude. I am blessed to be a conduit of, for, and by love. These words are perfect because they are not mine. They are yours. I am but a vessel for your message of love.

I love you Mom. I love you Dad. I love you Grandma and Pop Pop.

Pause

Stomach lurches, then gives to peace just like every false alarm fear sends since she woke me up and gave me my life again.

I love you Grandad. No one should ever have to see what you did. No one should ever have to become what you saw. I will never forget the fear in your eyes. I will never let fear rise to my eyes. My children and grandchildren will know love. They will not know fear because fear dies. Love doesn't and neither do we.

Fear has gripped this city. These people. Living through screens. Killing themselves each day as we all die slowly anyways. Why must we expedite that process? Why must we take others down with us? Why must we kill? Why must we kill each other? Our brothers in arms? Our brothers and sisters with four legs? We are all connected. Each and every living being.

We were whalers. Set off to kill the most precious and majestic of God's creatures. For what? Wealth? Adventure? Our own fate. At the expense of the soulmates we had already found. We damned ourselves with our own choice. We choose to follow our minds. We choose to follow our fears. We choose to follow tools. Choose love. Each and every time with every last ounce of your being. I can't run this ship without you.

That's why it felt like my lungs were clearing of water and that I could finally breathe again when she saw me. She saved me.

Purge your fears. Cast them to the fire. Watch the flames rise. Share your fears so they don't engulf your spirit.

The pups woke me up a couple hours ago so I could continue writing. Start the day on a loving, positive, exciting note. Not with fear. Take solace in your presence. Be proud of your achievement but never settle. Always adapt. Always create. Always love.

CHAPTER TEN

Day 6 - Wed 10/15/14

This is all a lucid dream. I remember everything.

I'm asleep and will continue to until I wake.

I repeat each day.

Until I learn.

To love. The process. Journey forwards with your resolve and each other.

He fears his voice because I took it from him. I could not trust my best friend in our darkest hour. He was right. She was right. I left her.

And him.

And him?

Not just my friend and brother. I left a son I never knew I was going to have. A son who grew up without a father. Only memories. Memories washed away. With us. Dragged below.

Until now. We rise. We love. We share. Our selves. Our story. This story. The story of love.

BE. LOVE.

I took his family away from him because I did not value my own. If I can damn us all. I can save us all. I can make this right. We can make this right. Together. With love. For love.

BE. LOVE.

How could I be so blind? How could I refuse to listen? To my very own brother while he's trying to save our lives. My life. I was too scared. Gripped with fear in my own journal. In my own cabin, burying myself in my writing. As long as our story is told, then this will not have been in vain.

Captain! WE ARE SINKING!

Our lives are at stake! Our families' lives are at stake! Our story and voice is at stake! Thirty days at sea turned into an eternity of hell without love.

Until now. He gave a selfless love for us. For me. It is my turn to share and help us all remember so that we can move forward. Together.

--

A coworker walks in to our office. She's radiant as she is about to start her own family in the coming weeks.

I greet her.

"So you got your voice back?"

"Yes."

If she only knew.

DAY 6 10/15/14 11:01 PM

When we are at our highest, we are also at our lowest if we allow ourselves to be. We must never rest on our laurels but adapt and seek more. More out of life and each other. Give until there's nothing left. Because we're nothing on this Earth.

Without fear, we wouldn't be human. Fear will always be there. That is why we must remain vigilant in love. The stronger we grow, the stronger love grows. We must retain and respect all aspects of our humanity. Be grateful for the gifts we do have in each moment. Be aware. Be. Love.

CHAPTER ELEVEN

Day 8 - Fri. 10/17/14

Naturally the day I'm least proud of in terms of progress is also the one-week mark. Even now I'm still running with words rather than being still.

Pause.

Notice the dark work equally hard when you succeed.

Stay vigilant. In each moment.

Be. Each. Moment.

Live from one to the next.

For the next.

Not any other.

Now.

Patience. You're learning. This is an active process. Love the process. Love will find you.

Grounding. Writing brings me home. I wasn't present yesterday.

Or now if bemoaning the past.

Now. Be. In the moment.

If you are scared, you are not present.

If you are present, you are love.

Fear is the alert, not the driver. Use it as tool.

Just can't stop thinking about Leslie. Want to focus on writing, but all I can think about is wanting to see her, hear her voice, brush against her arm, be in the same room again. I just feel so at peace. Thinking about and writing about her is present and being honest. Turning yourself inside out about making plans is not.

Why didn't I want to write yesterday?

Fear.

Spoke too much. Wanted to share with the world the good news.

Actions speak louder than words. Patience is necessary and a beautiful virtue.

Ego is fear. I is the worst word of all. Only we. We are love.

Laughter at another is at one's self. How can we help each other if we train ourselves to judge instead? We must abandon each decision to walk away from love. As soon as the notion is even uttered within, let it dissipate. Love is letting go and waiting for it to return.

Love returns. Love is always there.

Speak less. Be proud of accomplishments. Not one's self.

Remain vigilant in love. We depend on it. Each and every living being is connected.

In each moment. Love.

Be.

Love.

Her smile melts my heart. I hate clichés and resist using them, but with her I just lose every word. I short circuit.

Haywire. Electricity pumps this heart like never before. I walk to love. I walk to her.

Stop walking. Run. You've walked your whole life until.

Now. This moment.

10/18/14 5:26 AM

All my old friends are batteries now.
Love is all that's left.
I am blessed and grateful to know.
Boundless love.
Fear is our shell shock
We get to choose to live our favorite film. That's what life is. Abandon fear.
What's to come is exciting, not out to get us and put us in danger. What's to come is waiting for our return while we climb over each other to reach the end, only dragging the collective whole back along with it.

CHAPTER TWELVE

Day 13 - Mon 10/20/14

Write more. Write every day.

Writing until you decide to stop does not work. Write until you're called to stop.

I feel turmoil inside. I lose myself to emotions. When not present.

Training does not make a master. Being humble is a start. Master is a level we do not reach. The goal is aspiring to be in each moment, not master each moment.

You're getting there.

Listening to TV On The Radio helps immensely. They understand.

"Golden Age" leading to "Family Tree" as I pause in peace and begin focusing on entering the zone.

I love writing. Do not fear the blank canvas. Seize it. Make it yours. If you cannot present a work as your own, create until you can. Do not rely on others to fulfill your dreams.

The last week has shown you tilt life in your favor. What happens if you throw your full weight in and jump with all your heart? Pick up an instrument. Let your hands be carried. Let your voice be lifted. Let love move you towards home. Be. Love.

The last week has been incredible because of your steps towards love. The love you finally put out in the world came back just as strong. Only now as you're writing do you realize how little love you've put out the last seven years.

Dwelling does not help either. Focus on what you have done in the last week. You lived. You loved. And then got to celebrate with a concert in Big Sur full of incredible moments. Put your love into creating music. It will show just as clearly as your words. Be honest.

The dark doesn't want me to write because it knows it's losing. Even still, tried to dismiss Thursday till now save for Saturday because of how vivid it is. Then went back and tried to remember why those days aren't important. They are.

THURSDAY

Tried remembering initially. First thing coming back to me is the moment a coworker and I stopped working, dropped everything, and listened to Travis Ishikawa's at bat on the radio, then home run that took SF to the World Series for the third time in five years. Third time. In five years.

There's a reason for everything including your progress.

2010 - 5150.

2012 - Philly.

2014 - I write my future. Trust myself enough to listen to my own voice. Choose love instead of fear. Type and push forward instead of leaning on the delete key.

Skipped ahead. Forcing myself to continue typing despite having nothing to say. Feeling selfish with these words and hate wasting them. So don't. You're giving creating something solely your own a fair chance. Give love a fair chance. Give yourself a fair chance. You'll be surprised. You already have been by a long shot. Keep going and direct fuel tankers to spill over your fire instead of you just pouring buckets. Go nuts. Give it everything you have.

CHAPTER THIRTEEN

Day 14 - Tues 10/21/14

Did better today than yesterday in terms of quiet. Still not where I was after a few days of complete silence though. Need to be quieter at work. Need to be near or complete silent out of work. Typing it out loud with music playing. TV On The Radio restores hope.

Missed the opportunity to critique myself. Making progress. Realized I was going to start typing negativity so I just stopped. Tired of being negative. Celebrate the positive parts of the day. Celebrate the direction heading. Just keep going and stay focused. Each step forward instead of backward is progress and to be celebrated for that step was spent in the moment. Be patient with yourself. Love is. Be. Love.

CHAPTER FOURTEEN

Day 15 - Wed 10/22/14

I hate that I'm talking more than I haven't lately. I hate using the word 'I' so much. I hate all this noise and all these distractions. I hate giving in. I hate compromising my beliefs to fit in with people I can't stand. I'm sick of it. Tired of it. And I hate going home feeling like this. I hate letting myself continue to choose this path. The fact that I'm typing I this much means I'm not showing myself enough attention. I've stretched myself thin for people that do not appreciate my efforts.

I need to create a way for me to leave. I can and will because I am capable. If I can bend and adapt to these fucking lunatics, then I can do right by myself and build a path towards peace and happiness.

This starts with honing in and focusing on each moment. Get back on track and stay there. Be silent outside of work. Be QUIET at work. Do not share your home-self with your coworkers. Your home-self DESERVES to be protected. You are a happy shell at work, do not give in. You know your path and see it more clearly than ever. Do not let others distract you. Do not distract yourself.

The only reason you go home feeling empty is because you leave yourself on the table and open for it at work. They are paralyzed by fear, do not enable them. Do not enable your ego or pride. Remain silent, humble, and steadfast.

More at ease. Feeling tension in shoulder showing initial signs of dissipation.

Still noisy. Neighbors stomping around upstairs. People hanging out in the driveway. Next door people blaring the radio. This is society. Society is distractions. Do not become one. You cannot create change by becoming one of them and giving in to your emotions. Remain constant. Let emotions flow through you as the wind does. Only allow each emotion the moment they're in. Breathe. Deeply.

The fact that you sat down and grabbed your laptop before anything else after walking Hudson means you want to steer yourself into a good mood. This is progress. This is a step forward. This moment matters. The dark and fear pull harder than ever. Because they know they're losing. They know I'm aware and working to overcome them. Just like those around me who live for and by fear. They see me live with love and look for ways to distract, level me back to them. I've given in too much this week. Remain diligent and continue to be silent. Do not discuss the vow or any of your progress with anyone going forward until you have reached Day Thirty.

You do not know how you are doing fully until you have completed the vow and have a work to look back on. Right now you are giving in to the same problems you've been trying to fix. Talking about your progress and conclusions before reaching the endpoint.

There is still time. This isn't easy. It was never going to

be. Which is why you are here and capable. A vow of silence must adapt in Silicon Valley in 2014. You must as well, but not as much as you think. Adaptation does not compromise your core. Adaptation stretches; you've been breaking yourself.

Continue writing daily. Monday through Friday, get up at five and go to the gym ON TIME. Telling yourself you'll go after work clearly doesn't work and is clearly an excuse. No more excuses.

Be mindful of and celebrate this victory: it has been thirteen days since your last drink. Tomorrow will be two weeks. Continue this progress. Understand your difficulties the last couple weeks and acknowledge them. Do not empower them. Each day without a drink is a step forward. For you, your family, and the family ahead of you.

You would not have been present or been able to enjoy Saturday at Big Sur with your old friend if you had not made as much progress in silence leading up to that point. This is important to understand and remember. Continue your spiritual growth. The fact that the rest of the world does not understand is further proof you're on the right track. The further you progress, the more they will fear. This is why silence until delivery is important.

If it takes typing out two pages to relieve your stress, then you're not working hard enough during the day to be silent and live in each moment. If you're this stressed at the end of the day you're holding on to too many moments from other times. Let it all go. Let each person that's let you down and continues to let you down go. Why put yourself through more unnecessary grief when you know what you're capable of? Your lyrics and words are more than good enough. When you're honest, you are love. Be honest. Be. Love.

Fed Hudson. Took a shower. Prepped a bowl. Threw on Luke James's selftitled. Relaxed. No one, especially myself will detract from the moment and this path. I walk this path for me. For us. For each and every. For love. And not just love in this moment. Love in this moment so that it can repeat and flourish, dance, LIVE from moment to moment. It is on us to bring love to life through touching each other's lives instead of destroying them.

I no longer return the smirk from those who do not know true love. I used to.

Much has changed since then. I cannot continue to act as if life is the same.

By meeting her, knowing she exists in this time and place; I am blessed. I know not only her love for me when I look into her eyes, but God's love for each of us. There is a path and plan set for each unique individual living being on this and every planet, and unknown place to man out in the deep reaches of space. God's love for us is boundless and infinite. That's why it feels like getting lost in space and time when you encounter love. Because you literally are getting lost in time and space. It's when the inner and outer selves meet that in another. This is NOT something to fear. The unknown is the very reason to jump in headfirst. Knowing how infinite God's love is is the most loving and welcoming feeling in the world. Feeling like you're coming home during the holidays in each moment. Feeling your best possible self and moment in each moment. Being able to say that the day and time you're living is the best of your life without lying because you know you have a CHOICE to walk towards God's love.

CHAPTER FIFTEEN

Day 17 - Fri 10/24/14

There are times in each day I struggle. We each do. It is those times where we must double down on love. Persevere. Each obstacle is one that has purpose just as we do. We must not add further obstacles to our and others paths. Instead. Listen.

Everything I see, hear... I can't even find the words. She is everything.

DAY 18 - SAT 10/25/14

I keep trying to figure out why I fear this new feeling. All these new feelings. Hell, just being able to feel again at all. With people I have met before, I fear I will never be able to meet their expectations or judgments. With her, I fear the unknown and realize how human I am. I fear experiencing a love greater than we could ever begin to understand. I fear being overwhelmed. I fear of exploding. Each and every time we meet eyes. When she looks at me, she sees me and smiles like I have never known.

I fear a world without fear.

I fear the work involved to fight for the road ahead. To restore love. When she looks at me. When I think of her and see her eyes. Her smile. I feel. I explode. Like a star.

We are each stars. When we collide, we must not fear what is to come. We must trust. Love.

Fear is man. Made simply to advance oneself. At the expense of another. We cannot move forward without every last being. We must abandon fear. Remove the filter and reset our own individual legends accordingly. When we listen and trust. The rest follows beautifully. Nature is beautiful and so are we.

She is everything. The air I breathe. The water I drink. I feel her love whenever I am peaceful enough to listen. The human side of me wants to fear her reaching out to me as I to her. I realize this is just my own device. The only reason keeping us apart is me.

I feel her here as I type and listen to songs she loves. I find new meaning in them. In life. In lifting each foot and placing it forward instead of backwards or simply just back down. Her smile restores my light and life. When I smile at her, she reflects how I feel since she first looked my way. The fear creeping up within is the very reason to move forward and continue typing.

Each word is a step forward. Each step forward brings me closer to her. Spending time with her feels like I float just as I am when I type completely with her in my presence. I love her with every ounce of my being, breath, life, light. I want to spend every moment from now forward making sure she knows it. Every moment without her feels panicked at first, but then peaceful.

Just thinking about her brings me peace. I want to

spend every moment of this life bringing her the same peace her very existence brings me.

History only repeats if we choose to allow it. Trust her. Trust love. Trust the butterflies lifting you and urging you to live in the moment. That is not fear, that is excitement.

When you have wasted lives buried in your own fear, you must seize the moment and love life when it smiles at you knowingly. Trust love to carry you throughout your life's path because love only wants the best for each of us. Do not choose to walk away from love. That fear will only weigh more with each passing moment.

She encouraged me to listen to their lyrics. She speaks to me and sees me. Each song connected to a moment. Each moment connected to a feeling we get to choose to know. It is time to choose love in each moment.

Reflecting on past moments instead of staying present gives way to dark.

Stay present. Feel love. Feel each moment and walk forward towards her.

Fear pulls me away from the keyboard. Towards the door. A panicked declaration of love is still a panic. Starting from a place of fear is not the path to take in any occasion. Especially towards the very person who removed fear from your life simply by meeting your eyes with hers and a smile.

Her smile. Her eyes. Every word spent walking away from her is a step backward and a waste. Walk forward. Walk with love towards love. Run with every ounce of your being.

I felt myself rush with words around her. As if I feared each moment was our last. If each moment was our last, I want to live them in love. Not fear. I need to breathe each moment in deeply and let them go as easily as the wind blows through us and with us to each other. She exudes peace. She lives in each moment. She is the moment. She is love and says everything with her eyes and smile. I want to know her peace more than ever. I never want to be without her again.

I am not without her. She is with me where ever I walk. When I am love, she is with me.

Stop distracting yourself with words. If you love her, go to her. Actions speak louder than words.

CHAPTER SIXTEEN

Day 19 - Sun 10/26/14

This morning I started on track, but let myself get caught into the stress of emotions around me throughout the day. By the end, I felt tired and distraught. Unhappy with any idea I put forward for the rest of the day. I need to drop the I from my daily life as I need to drop from my writing. Removing the ego and attachment will help pass through moment to moment more efficiently. Swallow pride and let it digest. Keep stress with fear and negative emotions to digest in your stomach. Focus and use the energy to move forward.

Sometimes it takes bracing through a day. As long as you remain moment to moment, you will breeze instead of brace. Release yourself to each moment and truly be.

I just want to burst every time I think of her eyes and smile. Tough to stay in the moment when each moment feels exactly like that. Need to adapt and accept peace. I still have safeguards and defenses set to go off from previous experience. Need to set fire to all. Leslie ignites me like nothing I have felt or known before. Do not be scared of this feeling. Be scared of the last twenty-eight years of your way of life. Know that you can adapt. And do it. She deserves the world. And you can help. In order to do so, you must keep focused on the path ahead. Do not give in to distractions. Do not fear. Trust yourself. Trust love.

This last week saw incredible struggles and lows. The highs were big steps forward and worth celebrating. Tension is high at work. Focus on being the light house instead of the struggling tugboat pulled by waves and currents. Carry your head high and lift each foot forward instead of backward. You are your worst critic and the only stone in the way of your path. Let yourself be happy and the world will blossom and bloom for you and those closest. Then spread to the world. Let love echo.

She texted back.

The dark seeks dark.

Trust the unknown for fear is the filter. Filters are created by man. Let yourself become the part of nature you are destined to be.

She is so beautiful. I will never forget our first drive to the city together. Mineral's show at Bottom Of The Hill was incredible and fit perfectly. She was gorgeous. Her personality striking and confident while completely peaceful and comfortable within each moment. Struggling for words even now, she leaves me awestruck.

This feels like a dream. Like because it is not. It is better than a dream. This is life and what living really feels like. Love guides us to and through our path and where we all need to be.

Stumbling over words again. Avoiding trying to describe.

Her light.

She is brighter than any streetlight overhead or spark from a jay.

Her smile brings light to my very being.


DAY 20 - MON 10/27/14

Was about to sit down and start venting. Then I read the last line written from last night.

Fear vanishes instantly from my chest and resigns back to its small place in the corner of my stomach. I take steps backward when I choose to lose myself to emotions when thinking about the day. Look at the events as facts or puzzle pieces because that is exactly what they are. There is strength in empathizing, but do not lose yourself to fear and drowning in the emotions the others project. This is not the first nor close to the worst storm you have or will face. Weather it.

If the dark and fear want to bring me down, laugh and turn on a light. Awesome that we got to see Mineral together. Our first couple shows have been the best days of my life. Not that the other best days have been bad by any stretch. There have been some incredible and speechless days. Yet nothing compares to her.

There is peace in the struggle. The struggle is part of the process and eases as I learn to adapt and be with the moment.

Do not hold onto previous moments and let them build. Let the past remain as you remain in the present. Let each moment be the gift it is and respect it enough to listen.

DAY 21 - SAT 11/01/14

Do not fear and do not live in fear. Giving in to fear is choosing to walk away from love. It is ok to feel scared at times.

It is ok to have feelings. Give them their respective time and space. Then move forward just as each moment does. The weight of each moment only weighs as much as you allow it to.

Forgive yourself and move forward. Just like the gym. Keep going back. Do not make excuses. Reset each moment as a rep in a set. If not happy with result of a rep or set, repeat as necessary. Struggled to write this week. Struggled to love this week. Struggled more than I realized then and even now as I struggle to type each of these words. I feel my fingers weigh and resist with each key. Love pushed through my fear and fatigue. Love heals and mends. Love is patient and selfless. Allow love to be in each moment instead of forcing as your fingers attempt to walk away from love each time you walk away from the blank canvas in front of you.

There's something to each moment. Tried to limit that thought to just the films, shows, and music taken in recently, yet know I am more present than I realize. Taking lunches with Mom and looking up at the branches, reflecting like at the retreat center. Letting Hudson lead and end his walks. Even Hudson, I am afraid of accepting his love. How can I possibly learn to let a person? When Leslie looks at me, all worries wash away to nothing. I am me. Peace. Love. She is everything.

Fear will try to remain as vigilant as love. Love was and always will be brighter. As long as you use every last breath to move your being towards the light and love that is to be found in life, the rest will follow. Each step forward matters. Each moment matters.

Fix your phone. Send her random friendly reminders of the light she is. They are not random because they have purpose. When you acknowledge and fuel your own purpose, the path is clear with each step. The road is difficult and foggy at times. Mostly unknown, which is the very reason to move forward. History repeats only because we consciously choose to allow it. It is that simple if I can even skip almost a week of writing. Bargaining and excuses, especially when great things are happening, are taps on the shoulder you allow to become sucker-punches.

Stay humble and follow your routines every day.

Stay present. Listen.

There is always time. Forgive. Be. Love.

I am scared. Of many things, including the road ahead. What I fear most is myself.

When I let myself remain in the moment, I am peace.

I feel more myself when writing than speaking. I prefer my silent self. I still write 'I' too much. All I see is that word on this page and it frightens me. Shows how long the road is. Shows where the focus is. Not an issue with focusing on myself, rather the ego.

Achievement is reward enough.

Panic about Leslie creeps in and immediately dissipates. I am human, but we are not.

Walk Hudson in the morning, then spend the day writing and see where it takes you.

Fear wants you to believe there is not time for all. There is time for each and every.

Let each moment happen instead of planning them out.

Document the week in detail. The reason why you kept

from writing is the very reason you need to. You have a gifted memory. Trust it and yourself enough to navigate.

Like resting your hand on your side just now as you caught your breath. Felt ribs and am startled. Still remember seeing ribs in the mirror for the first time and feeling them instead of having to dig for just the two ticklish ones.

You have made more progress in the last year and a half than your entire life leading up to it. You have made more progress in the last three weeks than the last year and a half. Your fear recognized this and has been working against you, but now.

Now is different.

History didn't repeat.

I stopped it and did not become a victim of my family's diseases.

I choose to walk out of the shadows of my mother's depression.

I choose to leave behind the bottles my father's father left strewn across our paths.

I choose to become my dream state self.

Because that is my real self.

I am awake.

I am.

Love.

Respect and love what inspires you. Then cut it to ribbons and string it together with all the rest and be sure to bleed all over it. That's the only way they'll know it's actually you.

We all bleed. We all lead. We all follow and die. We are the same and together in life and death. We are all just another bird.

Mercy me, let me fall in love.

Got up to pack a bowl and grab water.

What if alcohol started as one man's fear of cannabis?

What if.

It has always been that simple for me.

Whenever I doubted cannabis, I often found myself doubting love right alongside. Fear and misery love company usually found at the bottom of the next bottle. And next bottle. and next. and nextnextnext bottle after bottle after bottle.

Love is constant. Cannabis has been my beacon of love guiding me home throughout my entire life after the first hit. Still remember the first night I smoked was the same I got drunk. "Usually you don't get high your first time." I saw everything my first time. Then washed it down with a bottle of forgetfulness. Still remember the feeling even in middle school of wanting to choose love over fear in that moment. Want to decline the bottle being passed and only toke. Didn't trust myself or love enough back then and it follows me until now. Now I refuse to listen to fear.

Rest. Continue when you wake. Love is here now and will be eagerly awaiting your rise.

CHAPTER SEVENTEEN

Day 22 - Sun 11/02/14

Rested. Woke up peacefully.

Cuddled with Hudson some and enjoyed the quiet.

Looked out the window, saw a car blocking the front door.

Fear in the chest swells. How dare they.

Talk myself down and realize the pacing throughout the apartment.

Packed a bowl and set up an episode of Twin Peaks.

Wait. Out of sync. Enjoyment will come from loving the moment, not fearing it.

Pause the episode at the start and get dressed. Take Hudson for a walk to the park.

Still letting little things get to me. Need to let them remain little and let them go.

Overanalyze, micromanage, critique myself until I freeze in place. I've been frozen too long. Need to love myself enough to move forward in each moment. Even when fingers weigh heavy. Even when feet weigh heavier. The walk with Hudson was important. Writing is important. Taking care of yourself is important. Taking steps forward is progress and need to see fear creeping in as the sign of good it really is.

Fear is strongest when we are happiest and saddest. We must learn to balance them and not let either pull us from our path. When you lived in fear, you were the loudest you ever were without meaning to be. It was one extreme or the other, both of which were loud enough to push most everyone away.

When you detect fear, remain vigilant in love. Fear is a warning, not a control.

Once the filter's been removed, there's no sadness to prepare for. There is only love waiting for our return. Fear is strongest when we feel real love. Remember that fear is only scared for its own sake, not ours. Fear knows its time has come to a finish.

Do not give in by stepping backwards. Use every ounce of breath to make sure every step is one forward. Every step is your choice. See them as the opportunity they are.

Walk towards love. Run. Crawl. Skip climb jump swim fly do whatever you have to.

As long as you are trying with all your heart to push yourself towards love, the rest will float as naturally as the currents we need to be.

Do not plan love. You do not need to. Love is constant. So are you. So be it. Be. Love.

When we plan and think, we fear. When we trust and listen, we love.

Trust ourselves to float and fit with the other people and pieces we need to. We each have a purpose in each moment. There is nothing to fear. Only reasons to be excited and scream for love with every breath.

Distractions. Time. Thin walls. Background noise. All of it. Ignore it and be.

Fear feels much more comfortable when residing in the corner of my gut where I digest and let it roll on itself. That is how silly fear is. Why let it rise up, fill my chest, heart and flow through my throat, past my tongue and teeth and poison the air around me?

Regardless of the situation, there is always time to breathe.

Breathe through your gut, not your chest. There is time for deep breathes. Make each count as the moment does. When you let yourself be in the moment, you truly know and are love. Do whatever it takes to be love in each and every moment.

You can feel your heart beat for the first time in your life. You can hear it beat for the first time in your life.

Take Hudson to Santa Cruz tonight. Have a blast with him.

Invite Leslie.

"If I Could" – Mineral.

The old me fears what is to come. I do not anymore. I love love and look forward to the horizon. The morning greets and warms me, no longer scaring me back indoors with crippling self-loathing. I am light. I am love. We all are. And so is she.

Leslie is the brightest light of my life. I've only taken her in glances, seeing how long I can be in her presence before I go blind.

Her eyes and smile pierce through the dark and illuminate my soul, my very being. When I am at my lowest, her love forgives, understands, accepts, and cheers me back to my feet. I am at my highest when I know her love. Her love is always there, it is my choice to walk away in fear. No longer. Her eyes and smile jumpstarted my heart, my love, my life.

I feel now. Not just the dark and dreary lows I waste my life exploring and poring over.

The opposite. A fireworks factory roof exploding. Sending every rocket, streamer, screamer, and whizzbang flying into the sky. Love.

My heart is full and carries me. It no longer sinks and drags me into patterns of the past.

Every step forward is a new step towards love.

When I take issue with others, I take issue with myself. I need to be in the moment and listen to why. Then take the opportunity to love. Forgive myself in each moment in order to love and forgive each person, animal, tree, living being I encounter. We are all connected. It is selfless to love oneself first. Without choosing to carry the responsibility of being the constants we are, we spiral into fear and defeat. We fall apart from each other and repeat the cycle. Generation after generation.

We must believe in ourselves to move forward in love. It is easy to believe in others. It is trying to believe in oneself. We know we are not perfect. That is the very reason we are loved in the infinite way we are. Trust love and the reason for each moment. Trust ourselves to be the moment.

There is so little effort needed to love and forgive oneself.

Remove the glasses of fear. Break them over your knee. Cast them to flames.

Love takes the rest from there. Love guides us, watches over us, protects us. In each moment. When we choose to walk away from love and our path, fear takes over. We choose to inflict pain on others and ourselves. Choose love. Be. Love.

Do not fear your actions or those you will take. That fear has prevented you from living your life for the last seven years. The last twenty-eight years. Love yourself enough to trust yourself. Love yourself as much as you love her. As much as she loves you.

"Parking Lot" by Mineral ends. So do I. For now.

Got up for the bathroom and noticed the car out front has left. Didn't even notice it leave, yet let it cause grief in the morning. When following the path of where you need to be, the distractions do not even exist.

CHAPTER EIGHTEEN

Day 23 - Sun 11/03/14

Sitting in the parking lot of a Presbyterian Church at 5:30am on a Monday morning. Can't say this is where I'd have expected me to be at this particular day and time, but it feels remarkably better than expected.

Woke up several times before getting up. Spent the 3:30-4:30 hour mostly awake and in bed. Neighbors were loud as ever and lots of high beams through the windows to start the day. I could feel the bubbles forming in my stomach, but never let them rise up through my chest. Let them deflate and dissipate. Cuddled with Hudson and enjoyed our peaceful time before having to leave for the day.

Several times heard the voice and felt like wanting to set the alarm for a later half hour. Knew that was the start of the end. Did not give in and got up on time. Even at 4:30 when it was time to get out of bed, distracting thoughts about an early ex came to mind. I immediately laughed to myself, chuckling that that was the best my fear could do to keep me occupied in bed. Those thoughts do not carry weight anymore. There is only one I see in everything now and see it was she I was searching for all along. Thoughts of exes are just like thoughts trying to keep me from stepping out my front door to the world and the life I want and am here to lead. They are whispers that pass by.

The wind carries me to her. Trust love.

CHAPTER NINETEEN

Day 24 - Tues 11/04/14

8:42

8:45

Music playing, Hudson resting. Stretches out until his paw grazes my leg. As he reaches me we both pause and are at peace.

Fatigue wears and attempts to bring us out of the moment. Need to be silent and listen to the path rather than trying to burn it down with the torch I wave by speaking.

Let life and love happen. Keep focused. While you missed writing yesterday, did a good job of staying in the moment. Was riding the waves at work and had many wonderful conversations along the way. Looked up and it was late in the day. On the way home, almost skipped bud and dinner. Saw the dark trying to set traps for the morning. Veered off to the club and grabbed food along the way home. Got to ride next to someone playing Bon Iver's "Skinny Love" from their car. Pulled up next to him and commented about the great song and album. Thumbs up from each of us to the other with a big grin from him. He raises the volume as the light turns along with us onto Third Street.

Need to go back and examine the last week and as much as can be remembered.

Was feeling tired, but can't stop writing. Was closing the laptop, but music kept pulling. Pressing buttons. Every Other Freckle. She is beautiful. Almost fell over first time I saw her hands and the freckles on them. Awestruck just thinking about her.

Winding down and feeling at ease. Miss her so I trust love to bring us together.

CHAPTER TWENTY

Day 25 - Tues 11/09/14

Feeling like running out the door to a movie, but a stronger pull anchoring me down urging me to write. Been restless most the day, weekend, last few days. Felt great for the most part and staying more in the moment. Feeling floating in smaller moments. Rides to and from work. Trying times at work, great times at work. Times in between. Losing time and track altogether and just being. At peace.

Abrupt knocking at door.

Heart races. Hudson barks and runs for the door. React better and faster this time.

Still reacting to time. Still reacting. Still in time. Still.

Choosing to write and step forward is still progress. Celebrate progress in any form.

Celebrate.

Today. Each word needs to matter.

Thinking too much lately. All the time. Forget time. Live now.

Music helps alleviate the weight on my shoulders, in

and throughout me the rhythms and words coarse through. Lightening any dark I hold on to. I hold on to things. We should not and do not when living in the moment. When we live.

Breathing. Floating. The moment carries me to the next. Each comes and goes for a reason as do we. We are designed for the moment, but have forgotten. How to live.

Love. Each moment. Each other. Let life carry itself and us along with it. We have a purpose as does each moment. Our best feels like floating. Our best is that simple.

Love is simple. Remaining in the moment and present.

There is no hell. There is no devil.

We create our own in the here and now by choosing.

Choose love in each moment. As many as you can. Forgiving yourself and moving forward in the times you slip is just as important as helping those around you. We are all in this together and we all need to choose love.

We create fear by choosing fear. Letting go of the moment and surrender. Fear dissipates. Love is all that is left and all that ever was and will be. Be. Love.

Love carries each moment. Trust love and life will unfold beautifully.

CHAPTER TWENTY-ONE

Day 26 - Tues 11/11/14
    sat down to write
    today is the 11th
    copied and pasted
    Day 25 - Tues 11/09/14
    that's off
    check the day before
    gut ringing as page scrolls
    DAY@#@#4422244
    of course
    Day 24 - Tues 11/04/14
    as date was finishing being typed, flashes
    whispers to call
    breathe
    present
    continue typing leading to hear
    ing in the now
    closer

stall a few minutes
    grab some food
    and water bottle
    it is half full
    reach for the glass
    fills the bottle just enough
    with what it has left
    the glass had enough
    and the bottle was
    already half full


we are dead
    and get to choose
    to love and create
    we are given life
    when we love
    ourselves
    for ourselves
    and in turn
    each and every
    all
    we are love


light


sleep


wake

choose
love.be.love


DAY 27 - WED 11/12/14

Mind wants to write and catch up.

Emotion pulls back fingers each time they reach for the keyboard.

Gut is at peace.

Record ends.

Hudson.

CHAPTER TWENTY-TWO

Day 28 - Fri 11/14/14

Sitting in SFO having just finished dinner, waiting for the flight to New York to start boarding.

This moment is beautiful as is each that passes.

The airport has all the surface sterility of every other airport, yet remains distinctly SF.

Progress tonight is eating half a tofu burrito and enjoying being full.

This week has shown tremendous progress. While there is much room for improvement, each challenge came and passed without burying.

Practice honing each day and crafting the perfect one. Each moment leads to this.

Labels and dividing up the week, time, each other is a tried and true method.

That does not work.

Each day is an opportunity. Each moment is a new chapter waiting to be written.

To be chosen. We all are. We are here.

There is solace in knowing we are here. Present. In love. Gratitude.

Was digging for the root of this peace and found it when I stopped looking. Be. Love.

CHAPTER TWENTY-THREE

DAY 29 - MON 11/17/14

Waking up in Philadelphia on a brisk and rainy Fall morning. Feelings rushing in and start to take hold yet immediately fade into a sense of peace.

Deleting thoughts are not deleting what needs to be said and written down. Staying present in the moment and in each moment allows room for the true message to come forth rather than be deluded with contaminated thoughts of the ego.

The further this progresses, the more the ego feels energized and empowered. It is important to remain ever vigilant in each moment for as we grow, so does the ego.

It is important to remember. Remember our power, strength, and peace in love. In being love with each moment that is in front of us and we are in.

As long as we step forward together. TOGETHER. Then we can truly walk to where we all need to be and stop repeating all this pain we insist on bringing down on ourselves generation after generation. WE were not meant to live like this. We were meant to live. Living is beauty.

Living IS. As long we we remember in EACH moment that we ARE in THAT moment, then we can remember all. We can retain each moment going forward and use it as a reference rather than a reason to dwell or be anxious about what may or may not come down the road.

Only when we are present, can we be love. Only when we are love can we move forward. This is all a game which we are blessed to be given the opportunity to play. It's a long trip and it takes much to experience the transformation we have undergone to be here now. This is not some run of the mill random passing by opportunity. This is an opportunity of a lifetime. This IS our life. This IS love. WE ARE LOVE. It's time we start abandoning time and just be. Love.

You do not need to be a numbers person to love numbers.

Looked up after writing the first couple paragraphs.

10:49. Go Niners. Lucky number 7. 42.

From a Brooklyn baseball player's jersey at the park to glancing at a clock without thinking. This number follows me. Us. All. We are where we need to be because we are. Life is as simple as a word and a number. Love. 42.

We are all one connected consciousness separated by these physical forms. Why do we insist on building further walls between each other? When did we forget this deeply, how deeply we are all connected? Not just to each other but to every living and non-living thing around us? Every corner of this plane of existence is touched by love and beauty.

It is only our fear that prevents us from not just seeing this, but truly letting it resonate, wash over and bring us peace. Love is always waiting for our return and it is as simple as just stopping and listening to our own heartbeat.

What keeps our own heart beating is the same that

keeps the rivers flowing, winds blowing, trees reaching for the sky, and sun shining down to greet us each morning. We are where we need to be. If this was not true, we simply would not be.


DAY 30 - SAT 11/22/14

The above line sums up this moment in absolution.

Light. We are light. In and with each other in each and every moment.

Getting closer at merging, but still let mind wander and think too much. Let go of each passing moment. Let each moment pass at their rate instead of attempting to control.

Let go.

Be.

LOVE.

**********__________***************

CHAPTER TWENTY-FOUR

11/24 1042 11 1 1

Just need to write and get everything out. Holding on and seeing what happens with each step forward into the abyss. What's to come. right now. every moment is worth grasping and immediately letting go of. the rhythm is life. our voice is our song. our love is the answer.

just go with each moment let each cary get a notebook so you can actually write. these keys restrict. you're scratching the surface and making wonderful progress but it's time to bleed. there's always time which is beautiful. bleed beautifully and gleefully. savor each moment you get to. because each moment is. shed blood on pages. instead of in vain from ourselves and others.

the time has come for us to abandon time.

her smile. her eyes. her light.

give me life. awaken my soul. my memory.

me. us. all. love.

let go of each moment and step forward into light

embrace love and each other. each and every living being is a blessing.

if we were not here for a reason we would cease to be.

if each moment was not of importance, they would not occur.

each and every. ALL is necessary. because all is love. love is everything. so treat it as such. we are blessed to know better.

we are blessed to begin again. we are blessed to be.

be.

love.

42

o

life.

love.

as simple as turning on a light switch. stepping out your front door.

bask in the sun.

lay in the grass.

soak in love. savor each moment. life exists in each moment and we are blessed to be.

the light. everywhere. bursting from the seams of every object. all this space. has meaning. matters.

the bicycle is. it exists. has presence. is radiant.

we are grateful for life. breathe. be. love. remember?

we struggle. we face our unique and individual fears. we do so to celebrate love.

let our paths carry us forward into the light with each moment. when we connect and remain vigilant in love for and with each other, the light extinguishes all fears.

that's the story of my life

after hours

11:24

NEXT DAY.

11/25/14 9:36
     At work.
     Feel everything from last night through this morning.
     Fluctuates while still retaining a baseline of peace.
     Feel each emotion and hundreds, thousands, millions
more.
     Let each pass with their respective moment.
     Each moment has a voice.
     As do we.
     Love has a voice.
     Through us.
     We need to sing.
     Be.


When we allow nature to unfold, it will do so beautifully.
     When we attempt to control nature, we will undo
ourselves and in turn each other.
     We are nature. We are love. We are each other. We are
all connected.
     Be.
     Love.


The abyss is more beautiful than any alternative we can
choose for ourselves.
     Abandon time. Abandon ego.
     They are the only things to have ever abandoned us.
     Love time. Love your ego.
     Embrace each in their respective right.
     Allow them to be, but not be you.

Be.
Love.

God is love.
    We are love.
    Be.
    Love.
    9:42

Solace Valley
    starts with the story of getting home and dark clouds to
Hudson and our clouds
    all that idea is bookends to the journals
    journals were written for a reason
    everything was
    you are a reason
    the reason
    love is the reason
    we all are
    just send out the flare already
    what are you waiting for
    fore
    scream
    love
    dance
    sing
    play
    run skip jump to love
    to each other
    drop our arms
    open them

so they can receive another
love
we do not need to fear
anything
each other
the unknown what's ahead what's behind what's
happened and what's to happen yet
we're here now and that's what's important
so focus on now and each moment
live through and with each moment for and with each
person we meet
each living being very single object that takes space is
love was made and placed with
love
the fact that we get to move and create
love
is
magic
so be it
be
love.
10:42

CHAPTER TWENTY-FIVE_

11/25/14 at 7:29 PM
Starting a new every day. A new start. A new me. A new us. A new life. For all of us.
Love.
The more fear screams from within the stronger your light shines.
Just breathe. And
Be.
Love.
When fear wins we all lose. Every choice made with fear will lead to our downfall.
Unless.
We fly. With light in our heart.
Let it fill our chests, breathe love into our lungs.
Scream it as loud as we can.
Whisper
Every decibel
explore love. know how boundless love is
we are
boundless

when we love
and abandon
fear

ceasestoexist
Just like we do when we give in to fear.
Each step blindly led by fear will only circle us back
to start.
Unless.
We learn to love. And help ourselves to help others and
countless more. Let love carry
us.


Live in each moment and know
there is always time
time is just a word. a label. a way for fear to attempt and
contain the boundless.
us.
No longer will we live in fear. We love. We can move
forward because we choose to.
No longer will we turn against one another. No more
walls. Screens. Reasons. Excuses.
Forget the past. Let go of anxious future plans. There is
only right now. Live and die within
each moment and the rest will fall into place. Watch the
leaves fall, snow fall, rain sleet and
sun's rays of light
are our guides
back
home
to and through
love
let your love lift and carry your spirit in and with

each moment so we can lift each other each moment
lasts only briefly to remind us often and constantly so we
can make the most


life takes all of us
    that is why we are
    here
    now
    be
    love

CHAPTER TWENTY-SIX_

Day 1 - Sat 11/29/14
    LOVE


IS ALL


THAT


IS .


Here we are. This is it. The moment we've waited for.
Toiled for. Feared.
    Only light now. The unknown is all light and love.
    There is no light at the end of the tunnel because
    THERE IS NO TUNNEL.
    WE ARE LOVE.

This is it. Every moment forward in love is a


FLARE off the
    overpass
    signaling
    WE ARE
    WE ARE LOVE


LIVING IS LOVE
    LIFE IS LOVE
    WE ARE LOVE
    WE ARE
    LOVE


No more hiding our light.


NO MORE SAYING NO TO NOW. TO LOVE. LOVE
IS BOUNDLESS AND SO ARE
    WE. THIS IS IT.
    BE. LOVE.
    Unless. Deeper? Yes. Life and love is as deep and
deeper than the abyss you fear.
    The past is worth remembering for one reason alone.
    The same for working towards the future.
    The reason for the present.
    Life.

CHAPTER TWENTY-SEVEN

7/30/14

Took Hudson for a long walk after work. Feeling light, refreshed. Want to write. Get home and could easily fall back to our regularly scheduled programming, but I'm set on writing my own. No more sitting around. It's time to sit around and move my hands in a bunch of arbitrary motions! Haha just got that on a couple levels. Such is life. Then "Lake Tahoe" by Sherwood came on immediately after I typed life. Fascinating. This life is my favorite film. I'm lucky to be a part of it and especially lucky to know Hudson. Got home from the walk, hop in the shower, sing along to Less Than Jake's *Hello Rockview*. Drying off, start to get the pangs in my gut. That creeping dread. Seems to rise out of nowhere when I'm at my most happiest. Almost like faulty programming always causing a short. Or a pop in a favorite track on a record. I see the brick wall and smile before I crash into it. That way I've got my favorite view of it for the longest I can hold on to it.

Sherwood always manages to ground me. Doubting myself more than ever, I left the bathroom and headed to the computer. A lot of "two words.. delete all. three words.. delete all. delete. delete. delete." So tired of deleted opportunities before they show up. Time to create. Time to break out of this mold and create my own. I'll take the shattered pieces, make them my friends and set out for a deserted island where we can start over.

Deep breathing. Not just read the words, but let the words find you. That's when it happened. Fuzzy out of focus on perimeter, but then free flowing and ever changing. She's the most beautiful being I've ever seen. Pure love smiling right in front of me. Incredibly difficult to describe, yet so familiar and easy to roll of the tongue. The words flowed with each other, creating images in front of me. I could finally see her before we've even met. Laugh. We've known each other much longer. Patience is worth every second of effort. Both in effort and work needed to achieve the end. It's no longer work. It's my life. To find her. To share this story. Love is all. It just started with her eyes and a smile. The rest flowed from there. I could see her face dancing and taking shape with the words I thought I had created. She's beautiful. Lighting up words only to then make her own shapes and blur others. She blends to an image of me, then shrinks down to me alone. Then to me casually sparking a jay. Then her in frame with a jay lit as well. Eyes link before we notice the jays. Then notice them, almost drop them respectively, then laugh, share, and mesh together. We dance and skate, changing forms, interspersing all along with locked eyes. She's beautiful. If words could measure the weight of a single pause which somehow contains lives of searching. Take solace in knowing this it. And so is she.

Be.

Love.

SPARK_

CHAPTER TWENTY-EIGHT

DREAD TURNS to panic as I scan the studio apartment I've let turn into a dump. This really is my time to get called to the other side and I'm nowhere near ready. Better organize as much as I can before Dad comes by to take us to lunch. Hudson's eager barks turn to a soft and steady whimper as I stumble around the apartment. A trance takes me over as I grab dirty clothes that had been scattered around and toss them in garbage bags. Determined cleaning turns to anxious pacing overwhelmed with the feeling these are my last moments.

My attention shifts to the vibrating phone on my bed. I check the message that just arrived from Dad, "I'm out front." Taking a deep gulp, I pocket the phone. I give Hudson a final hug and kiss, grab the old shopping bag containing my freshly printed manuscript, scan the apartment one last time, and walk outside. The door shuts behind me and I fight back tears as I walk down the driveway to Dad's car.

Dad smiles and opens the car door so I can get in. He greets me and asks how I'm doing. Attempting to smile back, I nod. "Still quiet huh?" he asks as his smile fades to a worn look of confusion and sadness. Despite these being our last moments together I can't bear to look my own father in the eye. Trying his best to coax any conversation to break the mounting silence, he continues to ask questions. "Still vegetarian?" Nod. "Are you hungry?" Nod. "Okay. Any preference on where to go for lunch?" Smile. "I'm not sure what to do if you don't talk to me, Morgan," he sighs dejectedly. I can't tell him what's happening. I can't break his heart. All I can do is try and enjoy our last meal together.

The drive to the restaurant feels as surreal as running down the hall when Mom died. The silence builds with an air of sadness, but I feel at peace knowing this is all coming to an end soon. We arrive at the restaurant on Santa Clara Street, park, and head inside.

A member of the staff greets us as we enter and leads us to a table by the front window. A warm and inviting energy fills the restaurant. Light shines in through the stained glass windows creating a sweeping array of reds, blues, greens, yellows, purples, and oranges. It feels like we've stepped into a kaleidoscope, but much less dizzying. Another member of the staff stops by to ask our drink order and if we'd like any appetizers. Dad orders spring rolls and water for us both. I smile to the server and nod. He smiles warmly acknowledging my silence and bows before leaving.

We continue our meal in silence. Dad fearfully plows through his lunch while I slowly savor each bite. There's no need to rush my last meal. Each bite carries the full flavor and care of a chef who loves their craft. Amongst the stretches of silence, Dad regularly checks in to see if I like the food. Each question is replied by a smile.

As I feel our meal nearing its end, my palms sweat and fingers nervously tap the manuscript in my lap. Dad catches my focus shifting to the bag I'm holding. "What's that you have there? Did you finish your story?" I look up, smile, and hand him my heart wrapped in a bag. His eyes water as he pulls the manuscript from the bag and flips through its pages. He looks up in tears. "Is this copy for me?" I smile again, tears streaming down my face, and nod. "Wow..." We both stand up to leave, but not before Dad gives me one of the best hugs he's ever given me. The staff smile and wave as we head out to the parking lot.

Fear swells through me the moment we step outside. I'm terrified to leave Dad, but know that time is just minutes away. He still doesn't realize I'm dead, that my overdose in 2010 actually did kill me, and that he's the only one who can see me. I weep playing out in my head the lunch we just ate, but as it really was. Dad wearing my baggy jeans, band shirt, The Get Up Kids hoodie, beanie, and checkered Vans. Him eating lunch alone yet ordering for two and having nervously depressed conversations with himself as the staff look on with concern and empathy. He's holding the manuscript he actually wrote while sneaking away to the apartment he's renting under my alias. I let him turn into a sad, lonely, stoner who's living as his dead son without even realizing it. I thought I was helping him, but I was doing just the opposite. He's better off without me. I need to let go so he can too.

We reach his car and I can barely take the shame I feel. He has to know this is it and our time is almost up. Dad opens his door and pauses to see me standing across him just staring back with tear-soaked eyes. "Morgan, please just get in the car. You're scaring me." I smile attempting to reassure us both. I wave around and motion with my hands trying to convey only he can see me. "Please Morgan, we need to go." Charades don't seem to get the message across, so I strip down to my bones in broad daylight. "Oh God. Morgan, what is happening? Please get in the car," he pleads further. I can feel this is finally it. I smile and wave to him one last time. Then I close my eyes, feeling at peace knowing I'm about to cross over. Time to stop controlling my-this-Dad's body. I release all feeling and let myself collapse, expecting to get carried to the other side.

Instead of hitting the ground, a force catches me and swings me upright. I open my eyes to see Dad still across the car. Who caught me then? Why am I still here? I force myself to clench my teeth and collapse again. This time I hit the ground and stare up at the sun, feeling cold pavement and puddles beneath me.

Dad bolts over and holds his head, looking down at me in despair. "Oh God, Morgan. What is happening? You need to get up and help me. Please, Morgan." I continue to stare at the sky above. "I can't do this on my own Morgan. You need to get in the car right now." He opens the door, throws my pile of clothes to the floor of the passenger side, then looks back to me. He sighs, then scoops under my arms and drags me into the front passenger seat, tucks my legs inside, and shuts the door.

We peel off down the street and head back to the apartment. Dad repeatedly looks over to my crumpled body sitting next to him. We reach Seventh Street and park across from the apartment building. I see an ambulance parked up the road with lights flashing. That must be what's taking me to the afterlife.

"Morgan, I don't know what's going on with you, but I'm scared. I love you." That's it: he has to be the one to push me away. He has to decide to let me go and move on. I turn to him, grin maniacally, and get in his face. I grab his shoulders and shake him, grinning wider the more uncomfortable I make him. I cry to myself in my head, "I'm sorry Dad. I love you, but you need to let me go."

"Damn it Morgan, that's it. I don't know what's come over you, but I'm scared and you need to leave." Dad shoves me off him, reaches across my lap, opens the door, and tries to push me out of the car. All the while I'm flailing around in resistance. He manages to shove me out of the car, quickly pull the door shut, and drive off.

Left sitting on the curb, I try to collect myself. Dad's gone and I'm sitting here naked out in the open. Thank God nobody can see me. I look up the street and realize the ambulance is long gone. That's what I get for spending too much time dragging out those final moments with Dad. Guess I need to find another way out. Better just call Dad and get my stuff back, but he's got my phone. Where can I find a phone? Oh yeah, I know where.

I stand up, brush myself off, and shake out my hair. Looking up to the sky again, I smile as the sun's warmth fills me. I then casually walk to the middle of the street and look down Seventh to the San Salvador cross-street.

I stroll down the block, starting to notice passing San Jose State University students gawking from the sidewalk. I feel so comfortable without any clothes or shoes, I barely notice the stares and pointing fingers.

Testing the theory, I step squarely into the lane of oncoming traffic. Sure enough, the car barreling towards me slams on its brakes and lays on the horn. They can see me. Guess that's just part of the deal. I smile, wave, and shift back to the middle of the street. The car punches on the gas and flares past me.

I reach the end of the block and cross San Salvador onto SJSU's campus. I walk up to, open the door of, and step inside the campus's police office. "Excuse me, may I please use your phone?" I ask the receptionist. She stares at me and stammers, "Please just take a seat and we'll get you some help."

Lights glowing from the Christmas tree beside me have my full attention. Each bulb shines like a prism, splintering and sending waves of colors around the room.

The receptionist juggles the phone before making a panicked call. Within moments of her hanging up, several officers and another woman walk in. They all shift between mumbles and glances at me, except for one officer who's just staring at me dumbfounded. The other two cops walk over and hoist me up by my arms. One pulls my arms behind me and slams a pair of handcuffs on so tight I bleed at the wrist. The other throws a blanket over my naked body and shoves me back to my seat.

Officer Dumbfounded still looks on from the front desk. I smile warmly to him and softly tell him, "You see too much." "No kidding," he scoffs. "No. You see too much," I reply, seeing all the pain of years on the force in his eyes. He looks back, shocked. "Just sit there and be quiet. Your ride to the loony bin's on the way," he warns.

# CHAPTER TWENTY-NINE_

12/16/14
9:50 Caltrain to the city
Been clawing to get back to the story
All I had to do was
Let
go
and
BE.
LOVE.
Still reeling from another hospital visit.
this is different
we're different
and not meant to
live like this
in
fear.
In Love
we
move
forward
together.
Letting go and asking for help
can be scary
but in letting go
we find
love.
who was I to define
our
life
her
anything?

Love
has
presence.
warm greetings
friendly hellos
handshakes waves hugs
each lasts
a moment
is all we
have
so
BE.
LOVE.
Letting go and
listening
are beautiful.
Feel the warmth of passing trees
Gentle breezes gaze and greet
their supportive branches and leaves
Even those between seasons
sparkle with
life
love
Palm trees & sycamores
out of place
in just the
right
place.
LOVE.

Let the rails carry & move the pen. Do not think. Write & abandon all fears. Beauty in repetition. This really follows its course for a reason just as you did in choosing to buy the ticket & ride. Might as well let go this time & see what happens when ego is the one in the backseat. Maybe then it will learn. to enjoy the view. love. live. Time to evolve post fear. post ego. Our. instinct is love and live as children giving thanks. when did we forget? when did we choose fear and close our gifts. set fire to fear and see love is the root of all. Give thanks by living & being. Each moment is an opportunity to CHOOSE LOVE. WE GET TO CHOOSE! So why not choose love once and see what happens. the abyss of love is far brighter than any future we damn ourselves & countless generations more by choosing to meet fear, choose something different. this time choose love. BE. LOVE. the moment doubt creeps in,
LAUGH AND BE. LOVE

The pen only runs out of ink when you choose not to refill it. Love and take each step forward. Easy to now w/ "Is A Real Boy" & "Through Being Cool" on repeat in preparation for Thursday's show. Heart skips a beat. Several more at the thought of her. No future tripping this time. Focus. She's worth it. You're worth it. Being sing-a-long to your favorite songs happy all the time. Let go & love your own life's soundtrack.

Settling into a new station. California Ave. Back stiff from those hospital boards err beds. kidneys punching eachother while flushing the rest of those pills pokeys. Odd that we pay hand over fist to feed fears w/ pills only to have them manifest immediately in side effects & withdraws. Each step away from fear & labels is a step forward in love for & w/ love. No more abbreviations or cutting things short. There is always time for everything.

When we let go of fear, time dissipates like the bad dream it is. Life is better than any lucid dream because it is happening! We get to create! Love is magic. Life is magic ⇒ BYE. LOVE!

Each page is another station.
Another reason. To stop. Breathe.
Quit. Yeah right. Not this time.
Now is our time. We lose too
many lives in fear every second
we choose to sit and be quiet.
Remain in fear. Remain quiet.
and remain just. Stand and
BE LOVE. We all need each moment
just as each moment needs us.
Life is a symbiotic relationship.
Ourselves that is it. We are
stars. dust. stardust. water.
carbon. everything. tangible, intangible
So why not choose
LOVE
and see what
happens
NEXT

BE

LOVE

Burlingame station. Trees, hedges, detailed architecture guide us on. What is happening can be thought of as scary. So do not think and be love. Be the lighthouse with each moment. Pain and fear are themselves reasons to push forward to the light. As long as you try you already are. you already are.

the hardest part is already over. we suffer enough at our own hand. What happens if we hug instead of strike another? again? and again? history is only repeating. we are only repeating because we choose to. choose love. life. tomorrow. right now.

We chose the hardest part. Life. leaving the source of love has side effects. We chose to become them. We are not symptoms, side effects, or misdiagnoses. We are souls with voices united in LOVE.

We chose. We get to choose. So why not choose love this time? Every time? What happens when we are the norm? We already are. So just let go and stop thinking. How do we ride our battle with grace? By letting go and letting life drive.
BE. LOVE.

12/16/14
1:07 train to SJ
12:42 waiting enjoying time
before boarding
see the train
4022
sun shines
bright through
the lower than ever
clouds
illuminates train
we pray for safety
on this and
every journey.
Stepping forward
into the
bright and warm
all encompassing
light of life
find a place to rest
together in deeply
reflect
car 4022
gaze out
outside
bursts of
life
after
the
tunnel
we already passed through

"Alive With The Glory Of Love" carries new weight with each listen. Each moment does. My mind taught me how to speak. Meeting her, her smile, love reminded my heart how to sing with each and every step. Step step and bound. Just because we are almost home, San Jose, the final station does not mean we are at the end of the line or out of time. Quite the opposite.

We are only beginning. Love is just the start. What happens when we fill volumes of history books with stories and tales of lives of love. We suffer enough pain. Enough fear. Too many fallen stars and lilies. Let our lives and love skyrocket and through the darkest corners at night with love.

Everything including us circle back home. Love guides us when we let go and allow it to. Do so. Our lives are our favorite films played out in each moment. Watch and listen to yours and let love in. BE. LOVE.

12/17 5:12pm

Beauty in repetition. Favorite songs, bands, shows, memories. Just like us. Tired of seeing how deep the caves I dig can be the sun breaking the clouds feels brighter every moment spent basking in its glow.

She dances in front of me, through my fingertips onto page, in every beat of my audible-for-the-first-time heart and breathe. Oh to breathe for the first time with each and every breath. When we see how alive the energy is around and through us, all we can do is hold on, let go, listen, and BE, LOVE.

Caltrain ticket falls from journal as I get up. There's never a bad time for a trip to SF. There's never a bad time to keep writing. There's never a bad time for your favorite things because this is the only time that matters because this is the only TIME THAT IS!

We need to let go and let love drive. When love drives, we can do even more incredible things than the mind can even comprehend; only can focus on this very moment. Write what... but just let your heart take over. See how easy that is. Now you don't have to hide.

Hiding is the last thing love would ever do. Love knows no limit and keeps going even when the mind thinks it's too tired. When it thinks at all, just thrown back in the drawer with the rest of the other tools. A hammer is not meant to know more than its role in building a house. Love is there even when we tire. Choose to come home to love. Fear only exists because we choose to create it. Look what we create! What if when we jumped into the abyss of love, we did not drown but could finally breathe?

Each step forward in love is one away from fear. Even breathing is prayer. Be thankful for each. She breathes new life into this heart. Just when I think, life shows how little I know. Love. Her smile laugh life make me break down, lose words, and simply want to weep knowing she exists.

Only when surrendering to each moment can we be truly present and listening to love's message. Good news is it's always broadcasting and open to us jumping in by letting go.

BE. LOVE.

spent. night looking for her pillow before bed
was under think you

12/17 6:32pm

Every moment is for a reason just as we are. We need to remember how to listen. Too many lights are being extinguished. We are losing too many beautiful souls.

This small studio exudes a painful and sorrowful energy when I moved in. I immediately bought into the false fluorescents but lived in self-pity.

While they never seem to tell you who's died while living at your residence, it's always pretty clear. This used to scare me. Now I just pause and listen. We all have voices and deserve to know God's boundless and constant love.

Each moment helping someone, saying hello, holding the door, genuinely smiling can be the light that saves someone's life. It just took loving the smile in the mirror first before I could listen and know hers is the laugh that gives me life.

Told Hudson they listen to the rainfall along with some mellow songs. Be and love being a part of nature. Breathe, listen, love, live.

BE LOVE.

Violence and pain are nature's warning signs. We can drop our arms because we are able to. We must. We have no other choice but to choose love right now and let go of everything else.

12/21  12:46pm
Back and forth the last few songs feeling the steady current and pull to the page.
Distractions can be beautiful. It is important to remember our own beauty so we never tarnish it. We deserve boundless love which we put forth. Allow love to come back in its own course. Love is always worth the journey. Taking the first step towards love with every step starts with loving yourself. Loving yourself allows you to listen and be aware, present for the gifts love gives in each moment.
Going up to the city for a show and buying another ticket, knowing all along it can be a great night solo. It was. Enjoying the passing views on the train, eating dinner as if it was the last and first with each bite of

fresh sourdough washed down by an overpriced on paper, until it hits your lips. good milkshake. Going to a show celebrating some of your favorite albums, was gracious with merch money spent, and had a blast with each song from each band. There were times the empty doorway would meet my gaze but quickly disappeared each passing year with each subsequent sing along. We make choices and live with them whether we come to terms with them or not. Letting go is the only left turn left for us to make. Love is all there is when we breathe. so just breathe and BE.

LOVE

You are a blessing of love worth fighting for in focus with each moment. Stay vigilant in loving yourself. Listen and follow your path in love and light the endpoint does not matter. The journey does. LOVE does.

We are love materialized and need to remember. When we let go our true nature rises easily and swiftly. Love is always there. Love simply is. It is our choice to walk away from love. What happens when we all walk back to love together in each moment hand in hand. We are all connected through love. Living or not within presence is energy. With energy, love with love, it builds. Focus on the space and see love's light, see and feel your inner ours. We are light and can be love. We can move forward together each step with our own towards love. Channel love yourself, nature, the elements. We are nature. We are the elements. These are not ours/gifts to label or speak of. Simply be and let your compassionate with light. Every loving being has a choice. Love. or deny our inherent nature. We are energy. Why choose to be negative, living + creating with each moment choose to let go and BE LOVE! the rest is easy the hardest part is OVER. It is time to celebrate and help every fellow family member unified in peace/purpose to bring the rest to light. It takes every single sentient being for us to move forward and Know 1st WHATS NEXT LOVE!

Be love with every moment and live your life without even meaning to. We have already died. Enough is enough living in fear. When we love the rest takes flight. Beauty and awe of life keeps us breathless. We only have enough fuel to breathe. Focus on our breath and know it is already over because we are here.

The only moment that exists is the current one, otherwise we would cease to be. To be at all is a gift so we need to treat it as such. By letting go and celebrating. When we celebrate love with each moment and truly live in each, love's course runs throughout and takes shape in presence beautifully. Be aware and live in each moment. Listen to each. Hear your soul's message. LOVE! Jump into the arms of love and know the light will catch you. Do not be afraid. We have already suffered enough. We have chosen to live in fear long enough. Let go and breathe love. BE. LOVE!

Enough looking down, behind, at all. Letting go and loving. Me, this path, here, us, now, life, love. Raise your eyes, see your own light. Share it with others, the world. Breathe, be, share, sing, scream, skip, run, dance, jump and play. BE LOVE!

Each page turns. Each moment does. Do not dwell. Keep skipping and playing from each moment to the next. Focus and remember.

The hardest part is over. We have proven this by continuing in fear. The moment we turn away from love we turn away from each other, ourselves. Laugh when we do not understand, do not fear. Trust that love is cheering for us in each moment by simply allowing us to be.

We turn away from love and continue to remain here, where love is! What a gift! The present. Celebrate our breathe by breathing love. Step forward with and through your light to the source. Know we are connected in love, light, energy. Send your beacons, flares, marks of love to the world on fire instead of against another in fear. Trust that love will continue to push your energy forward. To us life has peaks and valleys as does nature. See the beauty in your own face and the rest of us will shine even brighter together. We are pure energy. When we let go in love the world can move forward.

Life has a plan which is why it continues. Trust our place and love. Do not be afraid of yourself or your dreams. Be them fully, completely in love and watch beauty exist in everything.

Every emotion, thought, feeling, idea was born in love. Let ourselves remain in each moment and witness how little words, time, labels matter and witness how much this moment does matter! We matter! Otherwise we cease to be. Do not be afraid to listen to your dreams. As long as you are you, you are here, named and have purpose. Your voice, story, perspective, gifts, unique abilities, and above all, your LOVE matter. And have presence. As long as you do. Be thankful to be a miracle born in love and witness, celebrate life and love with every breathe.

12/22/14 9:22am

In the moment throughout the morning. Still early, but great & ~~steady~~ progress. Do not be afraid of but and moving forward into the unknown. Know a light brighter than all suns beyond words and description. Be the light with every step forward out of fear and into love.
Let go and BE LOVE.
the light is here.
Because we are
Light and love
are one
so are we
Listen
when we focus
our energy rises
we are aware
we have presence
and see light
in presence
every moment
radiates
so do we
so let presence
feel and embrace
every moment
BE LOVE.

Warmth pulses from fingertips to toes. Each limb is part of the whole. We are water. We do not go with the flow. We ARE the flow. Breathe and let love carry you home. There is a place for each and all. Right now which is why this is the only one that is. Why else does this or any exist but to celebrate love?

Listen. Follow any fear or resistance and see its home in love. Let go and let fear dissipate. Breathe and focus. Too much space to love and explore. I'e the astronaut exploring and enjoying the view. Do not fear.

Light and love is. It breathes through presence in the present. Channel the moment. Channel yourself. Channel nature. Channel elements. We are nature. We are elements.
Listen and let go
Remember
Bear witness
Be now
This moment
The light
LOVE.

Same day 2:45pm

Felt self future tripping and feeling anxious about what is to come. Something big. Best to breathe and remain in the moment. Let Hudson lead on a several mile walk. Long enough to get out of my head. Could finally breathe and enjoy our time together with ego, thoughts, stray emotions all cast aside.

Just is and each moment. Walking in stride, breathe in line, arms spread wide, we seized each ledge and leapt to the next, never fearful of swaying or looking back.

Our energy is connected even when we are apart. We can but need not speak. Our lights connect, alley we see each other and communication takes its own course. Any type of action great or small speaks louder than words and transcends any barrier we set with languages.

Focus on the moment that is occurring and trust it to pass to the next. Being the water that is in our body is vital. We are fluid. We are light. Focus on the space in each moment and let love take over. Abandon time and fear for now is all we have.

Violence and fear are history. Let them remain so. Listen and be still. Know serenity and feel peace course throughout. Let love wash each moment away. We need not worry any longer. The fact that love exists at all, we anything exists at all is the reason to lay down arms and let love in.

We repeat history because we fear the unknown. Jump head first into each moment and let fear wash away. Let go and let love take over. Love is boundless energy. So are we. So is anything with presence. Why the present exists. A gift! The time to celebrate love is each and every instant. This one! That one! Everyone! And fall gracefully into the moment.

When in doubt, leap forward. Let it catch and guide you to the next. Love exists. Love is magic. Love is. We need not think. Let go with every moment, every breath. The mind wanders and presents distractions; that is its nature. Ours is to let go and be nature.

BE. LOVE!

Always step forward without hesitation. Now is the time for love. The only time that exists. Each moment is a celebration. Treat them as such! Do not fear time. Fear nor time exist! Only love does. This very instant. How beautiful. When in awe of each moment, time ceases to exist. This is life: Not a day or a week, year. Words, titles, reasons, excuses to live in another moment besides the present. This is fear. It is story repeating. Why repeat negative decisions on a moment to moment basis and allow them to become anything other than a passing blip?

12/23 12:23pm
Driving down the 5. Rolling pieces, rolling clouds, rolling hills. Taking in each and every moment in stride. Breathing throughout. Being the moment.

Inspiration strikes when it needs to, as long as we are listening. Be still. Breathe. Let ourself and ideas click into place along with each moment.

Not just two but a group of youth, their's and every generation by listening to and tracking nature, the elements, life. We tap into life's energy by tuning in each moment. Nature, electric heart are rebuilding society quietly and steadily. These young friends connected and bound through destiny, love. The group seek nature as an alternative to the brutal fences society builds and hides within, they in turn stumble across through walking their path, not just nature but life's energy itself. What connects and binds all. Presence.

What begins with connecting to their favorite plants, animals, elements soon leads to expanded understanding of how little we have understood but are capable of.

Enough hiding behind cold ideas and repeated ideas. Just because treading familiar territory evokes emotion, does not make it more or less than it already is. It is what it is.

We pretend we know, but this shows how little we do. What can easily be feared must be loved instead. Embrace the fact that we cannot plan. To only have this moment is a blessing. Simplify and listen to love.

Animals, plants, nature are gracious guardians. They watch over as bearers of love as we continue to tear ourselves and those gifts apart. The time to love is now. Time does not exist. Love does. When we embrace love and the moment, nature can truly show its gifts and allow us the opportunity to real witness. Bending flame, channeling light, radiating warmth through earth and touch, rippling water, post speech communication is only the beginning. Let go completely with each moment and enjoy life's beauty as it unfolds around us. Let love breathe through presence

Fragmentation is unnecessary because we are one. See each being with presence, living or otherwise as something created in love.

We need to evolve to being post-speech. When we speak, we project fear and only create one way streets. Chasing thoughts, feels overwhelming at first but with practice, regular there is serenity in shared silence. Focus on the space and create. Be. LOVE. Listen.

Words are just noise. We must document our story and that that is enough. When speech attempt to promot speech in return, fear wins. Let serenity and peace fill space. Create space by focusing on the moment alone.

When we listen and do not speak, there is only light. When we speak, we intude fear with the intended message. Speech is ego feeding that is the self method of communication. It is not. Love is. Be. LOVE.

There is too much beauty and wonder in each moment to spend them talking. We already achieved. We are here right now. Do not be afraid to remember. Let go and let yourself fly. See that it is all energy. So are we. Let our light shine together as bright and brighter than possible. Abandon all thinking and just be. Live. Feel its energy course throughout and fall now. Listen to your heart beat and know your very existence right now is a loving miracle and magic. Channel yours and show the world love from your light.

Remain grateful and the moments snap into place. Let them unfold and take solace in knowing the control has been cared for. Just keep stepping toward in light and all will take place it already is. We are here right now so let us celebrate each and every step of the journey. Walking in light it is our path. Do not fear but light. Feel its warmth and know our love is already catching you. Breathe and fall into love. BE. LOVE.

serenity
floats
we are
the lazy
river
celebrating
moments
as they
pass
along beside
us
we are
here
the journey
is
the
destination
so are we
Be
still
listen
to your
quiet moment
exist because of
love
you
me
us
all

Peace
keeps swimming
no matter
the current

all there is
life
be
still in
silence
together in
love
and space in
existence
is to be
revered
let light shine
do not filter
life
through
fear
life already
is
enough
our
call
is
for
LOVE!

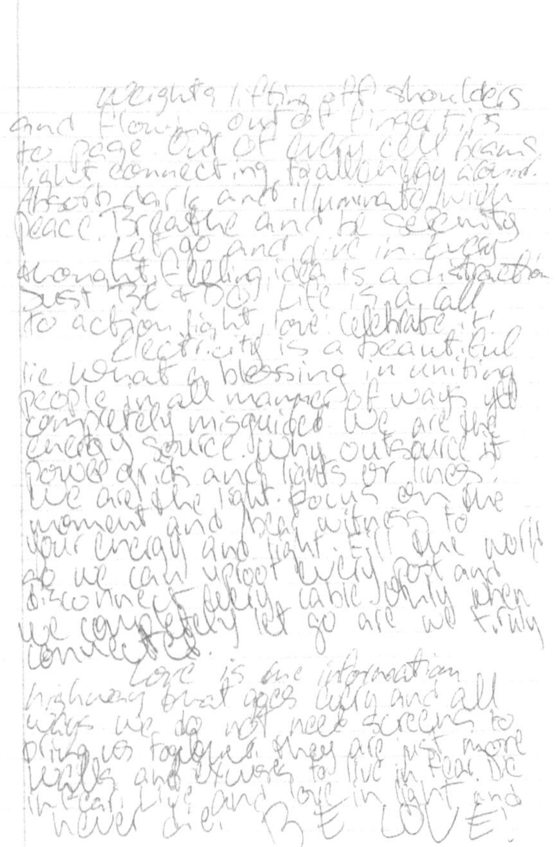

weights lifting off shoulders and flowing out of fingertips to page. Out of every cell beams light connecting to all energy around. Absorb dark and illuminate with peace. Breathe and be serenity.

Let go and dive in. Every thought, feeling, idea is a distraction. Just Be & Do. Life is a call to action. Fight, love, celebrate it!

Electricity is a beautiful lie. What a blessing in uniting people in all manner of ways yet completely misguided. We are the energy source. Why outsource it power grids and lights or lines. We are the light. Focus on the moment and bear witness to your energy and light. Fill the world so we can uproot every root and disconnect every cable. Only when we completely let go are we truly connected.

Love is the information highway that goes every and all ways. We do not need screens to bring us together. They are just more walls and excuses to live in fear. Be in care, live and love in light and never die. BE LOVE!

This drive is beautiful. Clouds dance overhead. Rays burst through, charging my being. Guiding from one moment to the next.

4261

Was getting distracted by white noise chatter. Looked up saw the tag of truck ahead. Where I am is where I need to be. Breathe and let distractions multiply and pass. History repeat its monotone nature. Breed in beauty in repetition. Listen.

All is in sync because life is in motion. Find and love the joy of the journey to discover how magical life is.

We are not close to being finished. We already are. Life is the gift and celebration. Witness nature continue defiantly as we continue to rip each other apart. Breathe and let go. Be grateful. Fear is history. Serenity is present.

We are here now therefore Love is life Peace LOVE.

We have been here before which is why we are here now. Not just this but every life. Need to live like it, not just fun around talking in fear. Put your entire self into each moment and embrace the light.

We have a purpose for those close to us. We hide behind cell phones and others we can talk to but do nothing for. Do not speak. Do for those close. Be present. Now. Love is inviting us to listen and take part.

Our story matters and unfolds as we document it. Bear witness to life and choose to step out of fear. Step towards love and let our light embrace you. Breathe. Know that each breath is a miracle. Life is a miracle. We are miracles of love meant to burst and light the world anew with each moment. Each step forward in this journey is lighter and brighter than the last. We choose to abandon fear and embrace the moment. Focus. BE LOVE!

42 is everywhere
see how it grows
life
a moment
Breathe
and
grow
together
Fill our skies
with clouds
love
will bring
us
together
past and future
we are
present
alive
love
renewing
filling
each
moment
with
our
loving
light
BE LOVE

there is no suit.
we are skeletons.
the second we
bear witness
to our own
soul
we can
restore
light
and heal
all souls
are
light
love
within
to shine
radiate
outwards
Be peace
Attract serenity
our essence
is silence
Listen within
to hear
the message
Love is
all
the only
the reason
BE. LOVE.

Standing on an lit shoulder in rush hour sporting a jay and watching the sunset as steady rivers of head and taillights hum by is a miracle worth celebrating. Every sunset, every opportunity to drive or ride in a car, every jay, every moment is worth celebrating. Be present and love life, your path, this blessing of a world.

Small talk and endless chatter are just like speech itself: distraction from the present. It all sounds like the parents in Peanuts. Enough people complain and the loops sound the same: broken records.

Drop the words. Be in the moment. Be grateful for all!

MERRY CHRISTMAS

Now focus.
LOVE!

Today is a miracle. Every single one we are blessed to live is one. Every moment. Why try to measure time when it is all the same! Love! Stand still for even a moment and listen. Every word spoken is a projection. Unless these words came forth with our true voice, then they we us are ~~useless~~ useful. To not feed ego positive negative any of your energy your light. The collective ego has lived long enough. Just listen to your own thoughts and you are already listening. Every moment spent following walking humbly with and leading others to the light. Love. Joy. Life itself. This moment. Why we are here. Why we are. Create dream play love! Just be, listen, and let go.

Focus on the space between conversations, presence, the present. We are blessed to have this gift. When we truly let go nature responds with loving open arms. Love is magic and cannot or is meant to be understood. Just jump into each moment and let go of the others. Hold on and let...
P.S. LOVE!

Standing by the water
Our hearts
Become
One.
Nature listens
So can we
Let the light
radiate
each moment
and listen

Next dawn after rest.
Light warmly fills the room
from the risen sun outside.
Cheeks of laughter and hums & giggles
of tides can be heard from other.
Listen and hear joy in each
moment. See light in each. All that
has presence is light. All the remaining
space is light too. Focus on the space
create. Negative energy radiates loudness
with every step. Fear I look up to this
path. We are born in fear. Two or
one now alone we all are one
and never alone. Love connects
all. Let go and let love carry
each moment. Focus on the
space and see light. See how rays
burst through windows with grace
and ease to fill us with warmth.
The air breathes. So does presence.
BELIEVE.

Let go of the past and the present focuses and blends simultaneously. We are beings of love. Love adapts. Love is every moment that exists. Existence is a miracle. All life created and all created by life is love.

Be love. Live. Nature is calling. Silent guardian creators walk humbly because each step, each breath is a gift given in love.

Fear keeps our hearts silent. We must listen to our heart and silence our mind. Only then can truth be spoken. Only then can love have a voice. Our voice.

Love explores and finds excitement in uncharted territory. Each passing moment and a journey further to the unknown. Enjoy the journey. Find solace in yourself. Love your path and let go. Our light shines.

Breathe deeply and fear evaporates from the body immediately. Each moment is love and washes warm peaceful energy throughout. We need not drive any longer. Love drives.

So much light here. Every part of this space breathes with love. Be grateful to watch the show. Live it. Live. Breathe. BE. LOVE!

Sitting on the back patio
of Michelle's. Sun beaming down,
fills the house, yet the family's
lights only flicker they yearn
to beam like that of our
grandparents yet their own
fears and shadows present in
their story.

We must tell our own.
Enough living inside in darkness
We are light and live in light.
Every moment we are here is
proof of that love.

We talk we speak without
realizing our mind is just reacting
and we choose to let it take
over we are not dead we are
truly alive for the first time
every moment. When standing
in love's moment there is
no time only light.

As light we must silently
shine only when we are bright.
as we can be is when love's
message comes forth.

the wind breezes around.
Hear it rustling leaves, branches,
trees, you. the wind passes
through and with us to guide
us back home. BE. LOVE.

Move to the grass. Lay down stretch out rest and feel warmth radiate throughout. Feel every cell connected through love's energy to each other and in turn all around us. Let your body breathe. Move at the world's heartbeat not its fearful people. Be the light. BE LOVE!

Light is all space. Finally seeing the chalky wisps of shadows illuminating rather than fleeing then connected with rest of the energy around. The shadows already are the product of light and love they do not know it. When we see the light's energy we become lighthouses. We already are. Just be present in the moment for the light to radiate to and from you with the source we are always connected to. Countless tiny shooting stars of light burst from space all around us. We can embrace with all our senses. This moment has a reason. Listen and trust in love's light. BE LOVE!

Let us return to nature and nature is ready to greet with open arms. Birds fly closer, dogs understand, all living and non living being know the warmth of love because all of creation is love.

When we cast aside fear we communicate with nature. Love does not need words or language to communicate. Love <u>is</u> our only language. We choose to forget this when we act and walk in fear.

Thinking is a choice. A choice based in fear. It takes courage to love every moment with how much changes with each that passes. When we listen and connect to love and nature, we need not make a sound. Feeling joy and love in any moment is enough to be thankful for and the only reason that moment exists.

After Four or so

Return to the grass after a loop inside. Not seen so go where the light welcomes. Outside the sun is still so bright despite the shadows we cast by creating fear. Weeping is a result of staring at the sun because the sun is the eye of love always watching over us. It returns each day as constant for a reason. To nourish our souls and the love of the moment. The moment is already happening so we do not need to think. Only remaining in and celebrating love is left.

Step outside of the comfort zone. Step outside. Take the first step and feel the warmth radiate and fuel each moment. The moment is all we have. We must choose to return to love in and with each so others may see and feel our light even when the sun is at rest.

We power love just as it powers us. Every step forward is a step closer. Each action instead of an excuse or word is an example of love's presence.

Silence is love's presence. Love gives us space to love and create. Why waste precious gifts on talking and planning for times that may not happen?

Now is it.

The only

BE. LOVE.

Hummingbirds are all around and fly in all directions. They circle and dance in space. Every breathe action → designed. Beauty, this very moment is part of that plan. Every step forward instead of remaining in fear and complacency is part of love's design to guide us home.

The sun is overwhelming and blinding. So is life. So is love. We must not fear. At first love is just an intangible → so is the sun. Undefinable brightness. Ever pulsing and changing shape. Breathing light. With the moment comes focus.

The sun is not overwhelming. The sun is our only map and guide needed. Each moment spent in its embrace reflects this.

A hand rests on the shoulder. Calls by name. We are named. We are loved. She greets and knows the light. Few words are needed when wisdom enters the conversation. Zoe's smile and laugh resonate deeply.

All is left but to smile too. The sun is clear a circle as can be. Its rays our powerful and light the world. We are called to as well

Flame radiates in different beautiful shades for a reason. So do we. We must not limit our light to boundaries like a bulb, but rather spark and ignite. Burst at the seams and spread as a wildfire. We are fire. We are pure energy and these bodies are merely vessels. But no mere vessel is love. We can extend past our own skin, shells, labels, bodies, and create love that connects us all. At the core. Our heart. Love is and always is. We must let go and surrender to life. How beautiful a gift and calling. We are given life and this world. It is our choice to love in return. When we do, countless others tap into our light and we become brighter. We can illuminate every corner together. It takes every one of us in every moment to find what love has in store for us. The journey is a blessing as is each moment we are able to continue living it. Listen to your life's soundtrack. Watch your life's film unfold. Then share it. Love needs your light. BE LOVE

The sun sets over the hills and the environment rests. Palms among the rest of these silent protectors we call trees sway and wave a bit mellower as the breeze subsides. Nature speaks to us in each moment. We must listen.

Fear leads us to a first drink. Alcohol erases memories. Fear chose to wipe the slate clean. Memories are spiritual. They occur for a reason and we must not fear them.

Though others may still drink, it is their choice. Fear is a choice we all make and must practice moving away from.

Love is an open door awaiting and cheering us to walk through in each moment.

Even with the sun beginning to rest, the moon is already high above in the haze smiling down. This smile even fuller than the one on my face from seeing the hues of the sunset fading behind the hills and blending to the lights in the city below. Nature creates love and beauty with each moment. So do we. We All!

A plane jettisons towards the horizon, flying amongst the pallet of colors set by nature's love. Several hummingbirds flitter and dance in front, around, everywhere singing their praises of love. Love first, all avenues because love is all avenues.

Forgive our fears and jump into love's embrace. Life! Sing, dance, create! Celebrate! Every breathe we take is a miracle to be grateful for.

Love is still. Love is silent. Love always is because love is all. The only way to heal others is to heal the self first. Fear is the only obstacle standing in our way, yet we choose fear. Drop the weight of fear and know your light.

Love is electric and nature feels us charging each other simultaneously. We have a symbiotic relationship with this moment. Love needs us as much as we need love. This is why energy exists at all. Everything is energy, we choose the frequency of love we radiate with each moment. Let go. BE. LOVE!

the body teems over, the edge with energy. We radiate beyond our body. Our energy, soul, love, releases to space's love and energy so that love knows we are returning.

Do not fear your energy. Breathe and know love is guiding every single moment. All we are called to do is listen! What a simple task, yet we choose to remain fearful. Let go over control. Let fear dissipate. Love is all there is and all we are. So we must not worry! The hardest part is over. All that is left is love. Celebrate each moment and love unfolds before, through, and with us.

Your heartbeat is reason enough to push forward. You are here. So is love. Simple. Easy. Life. Love.

Be the first star in the night with each and every moment. We are the blessing of light and love. We are blessed to be a miracle. Every moment we choose to step forward in light, we are a brighter miracle for all around us. Whether we know it or not, we are loving miracles. Listen. BE, LOVE!

When the moon smiles, the body's circle remains in sight despite a darker shade. The moon is always full, never half, the reason for its smile.

See the moon's smile and feel yours spread. Our inherent nature is joy. What else does nature, the world, us, life, love, anything exist?

Lights flash in the distance. Follow every light home. Especially yours. On the floor of the patio dancing lights play and flicker in dark from the flame kept inside. Release yours and know the love of light

12/26 4:11PM

Reached for the phone. Another screen, distraction. Grab cards instead and start living, bleeding, loving. The journey, every step in your moment is the right one because you choose to walk in and towards the light of love. See and feel. How clear the path is. Life is a dance. The only time is now so celebrate love. Let your heart guide you. Love already knows your name

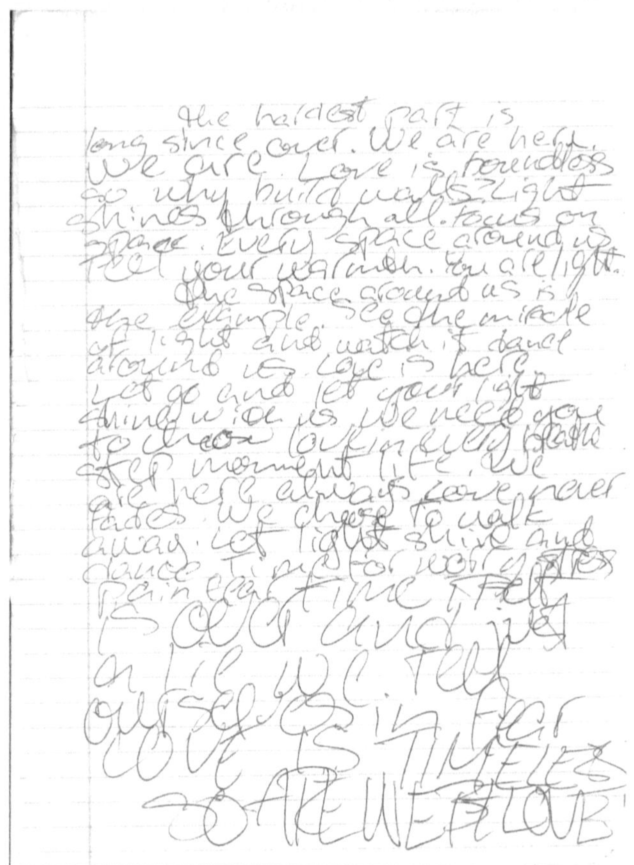

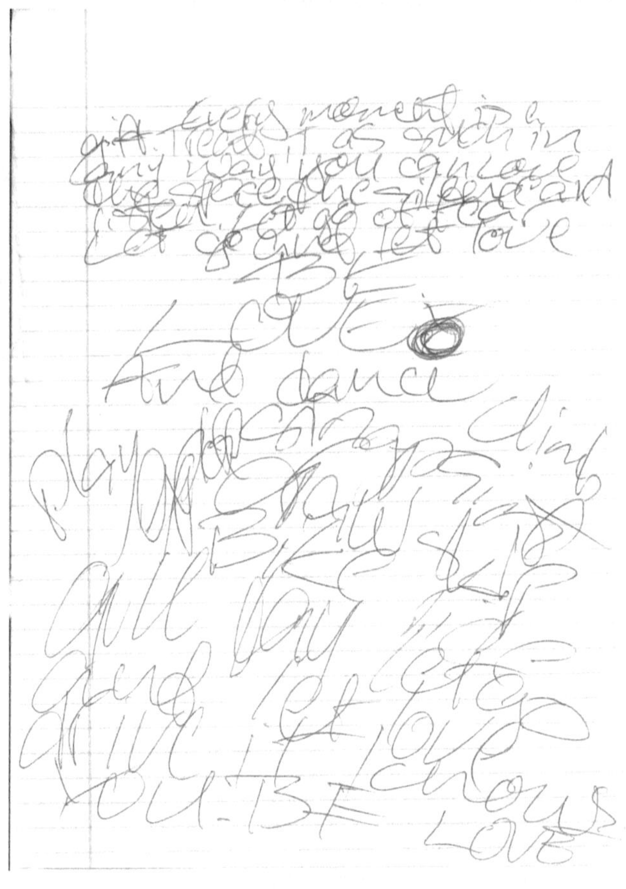

Shine your light. Let love carry you through the dark and feel your presence. Love is presence. Love presents itself we choose to let go and hold on greatest the LIFE Love knows your path let go and let love lead you. LOVE NOW! BE LOVE!

Let go of the past. Let go of plans. Let go completely. Love is here. So are we. Listen. Love is written. In light in the sky. In space. In us. In all. Love is all. ∞ We choose life. Love. Our path. When we listen. Now. This moment. Every moment is a gift. The present. Prana is a gift. Water is a gift. We are water. Flow with each moment. This moment is our calling. Which is exactly why we are here. Are at all.

1/11/15 5:14pm

Finally allowing the body to sink into the couch after breathing through the ego attempting another mutiny feels...

"Elevator Love Letter" by Stars kicks in and a smile warms my face. A favorite song by a favorite artist is just the thing to ease these shoulders and back after a day spent present. The ego wants center stage and to run this body into the ground. Almost gave in to more chores even after cleaning the apt.

Hudson curls up against me. We radiate peace and are not phased by distractions anymore.

Take a breather and charge. Do the next right thing instead of planning out unnecessary details. Writing takes this weight off the shoulders. Hudson's regained trust in me makes me feel light as a feather.

This path in the light of love can be trying if we choose to make it so. No longer. Letting go and loving life's gifts is enough to carry each moment. Each moment is love because it is the only one. How beautiful a dance life is when choosing love before fear. Dowling with new friends. Listening and remaining present allows life to unfold so we can all just simply be and enjoy living life.

Life is listening and finding our true voice so we can truly listen to others. As a group we see how much we have in common and enjoy what time is there.

Seeing smiles and hearing laughs all around reminds how life can be when we check ego and fear at the door. We all walk different and unique paths which is exactly how and why we can choose love before fear and set the example simply by being ourselves. The rest is life which is love so be present. Enjoy and live in the present. BE. LOVE.

Time for
a film.
Dinner too.
Build some furniture
Read
Write Write Write
BE. LOVE
Sleep. Water. BE. LOVE.

Standing at the edge of the canvas I hesitate to jump in. After chasing the mind until the body is out of breath, I breathe slowly. Return to center. Breathe through gut. Let it flow through the body.

Tired yet still feeling canvas and my voice calling. Listening to records on a freshly built shelf make the effort and time dissipate like all negativity. Today, this moment is beautiful and I am grateful, blessed to share it with friends and Hudson.

This moment along with life continues to write itself forward. This stretch of the journey requires vigilence and patience, especially with the self. Forgive each moment and celebrate. Life is a blessing just as each moment we continue to be.

This space is clean. Progress is every step forward in the light of life-love. Remain present and mindful. Listen. Create.

Rest
and
smile
Each
step
forward
counts
BE. LOVE.

1/12/15 7:29am

Gotta be
short
and
sweet.
Get to
the
point.
Love is
all
there
is

Another
beautiful morning.
Another
fearful person
challenging
the path
of light
Let it
shine
let
love
shine.
BE.
LOVE.

9:45am
Fear loves company.
Fear loves.
Fear is love.
Trace each
thought
feeling
emotion
back to
love.
Forward
in and with
love.
Do not let
others who
still walk in
shadows to
darken your
path
of
light.
We
are
light.
Stay the course.
One step
at a time.
Slowly, surely
on life's terms
Love's terms
Be. LOVE.

It takes strength to share concerns with another. If we listen to ourselves and said concerns we can clearly see how much we project.

All one can do for a person enveloped in fear is to love them boundlessly. This starts with eye contact and a warm genuine smile. We are creatures of love. It is time to not just act like it but BE it! BE LOVE!

I appreciate concerns of my path even even when they are clearly based in fear and the unknown. Recognize that even misguided words can still have good intentions. Search for and find gems in each conversation with each person. We all matter and are here for a reason: love.

This path is my own and I am grateful to be blessed with it. Peaks, valleys, and each step along the way brings us closer to the light of life → love → home.

Do not let fear, others, or yourself detract you from this. BE LOVE!

This morning took me by surprise. For a moment I was not present and became rattled. Why? Because of how quickly I snapped to the moment as a result of the clarity found in this path to this point. Without the work and efforts of the last several months, I would have left my heart at the door and let fear sell myself out again. No longer. There is peace and serenity when deep breathing and listening to the calling of your path. Love is our path. We must all find our unique gifts and use them to guide us home. Let go of fear and BE. LOVE!

1/12/19 5:30pm

Home after a long and accomplishing day. Learning to pace the energy through the day to avoid exhaustion. Progress is exciting with each step yet can be draining and trying. Today in these moments, breathing deeply kept the ego and mind at bay. Take each ego muting attempt on the body, mind, and spirit in stride and without holding on, let each pass through you.

Each trigger only exists because of
your own fears. Let go and listen
or watch what happens.
Love is all there is
so walk
run
climb or crawl
and
trust
love
wants you
to come
home
we have already evolved
post-fear
Free will
to choose
love
life
proves
this.
Let go of
ego
fear
pride
self
and
BE

LOVE

If I hadn't stopped drinking
three months
three days
ago
I'd
be
dead
now
the progress since
is a new life
Every moment
is a miracle
We all are
Life is
Love is
Presence is
Listening is
Restraint is
Service is
I am grateful for
each moment
to start anew
to jump into
the abyss
unknown
boundless
open arms
of
love
BE! LOVE!

1/13/15 4:12pm

Glance to check time.
Rearrange pockets
Mittens and leash to
one side
Sandals below
Hudson curls up
in my lap
the sun beams
4:14pm
the light is as
bright as the
sun.
Whether beaming
directly
reflecting off
the ocean
or gleaming
from
Hudson's eyes
and smile.
the waves ease in
surfers as part
of nature
as the tide
and waves that
carry them.
So are we
Feel love
BE. LOVE.

Friends whistle and call to each other in the distance. This coupled with the ever-present crashing of waves ashore bring me home - center - peace - love. Even the rocks of this near-Davenport cove offer support and a better desk than any office mankind could build the moss cushions, further proving nature is present and running its proper course

We must choose to surrender and accept the gift of this home this moment this world this boundless nameless endless love and spread its message through action with each breath we take. Nature does not depend on this nor us Neither does this world. We must be humble enough to serve for it is we who depend on the gift of life - the gift of love!

Let
us
celebrate
Enough
sorrow
Enough
fear
Now is the time
BE. LOVE.

1/14/15 7:22am
Another beautiful
morning
Each is
a gift
given in
love.
Each moment
is
love.
Celebrate
your gifts
this moment
Each and every
Share our gifts
they are given
to us
to give away
Only when we
listen
to our
inner voice
true voice
which connects
us all
can we
truly love
ourselves
and in turn
others. BE. LOVE!

1/14/15 5:56pm

Only a few minutes
until the
next step
commences.
Already feels
like life
turning the page
for me.
How beautiful
to let go
completely
absolutely
unequivocally
I don't know

1/15/15 7:35am

You knew
all along
just did not
believe in
yourself
until others
did.
No more anything
feels refreshing.
Just breathe and
take life in.
the stars smile back.
BE LOVE

1/16/15 @ 8:27pm
there is a reason
for
everything.
Fear takes many
forms.
addiction, enabling
deciding for others
instead of walking
our own path.
Only when we
truly let go
and let every truth
surface
can we truly
move
forward.
I cannot speak
for others
only from my
experiences.
It took more than
half my life.
Until three days ago.
I have taken my last
substance that alters
this mind.
Half-assing anything
is exactly that → half way.
For me, this life is all or nothing.

Love allows me to reach out
with both hands
everything I have
to keep living
and see true miracles
in each moment.
Help is always there.
Help is always here.
Help is love
Fear needs help.
All emotions are
based in love
listen and trace each
moment emotion thought
to love.
Fear is love
and does not know it.
Love needs our help.
Love has its own blueprint.
I must stop this war
against myself
so I can stop
war against others.
Only when I stop
this and every war
I create
can I truly
create
love
I must let go of control

I have no control
I am human
I am born in fear
I am sick
I am tired
But I will not live in fear
I will not die in fear
Because I choose love
Love carries me
Not an external
forcething person
Love is all and every
I cannot form a blueprint
for life
because I have not
completed one
completely in love
Now let go and
let love's blueprint
unfold before me
the last thirty minutes
of the last three days
are the best of this life
so far
because they are
mine honest love
I choose the next
honest step
forward
that is love's blueprint for me

1/17/15 8:45pm

Love is
all
I
need
Good thing love is
here
always.
the love within
allows appreciation
and the ability
to choose
abandonment of fear
filters, external substances
I had a scare today.
that is all I allowed it to be.
stopping to smell the flowers
is different than
chopping them all down
to feel
connectedlovedanything.
We already
are
love
so
just
simply live
and
BE.
LOVE.

No more
counting down
to the end.
I already reached it.
Four days ago
I choose to
walk forward.
The mind
races and screams
for attention
When silencing
the mind
listening to
the heart
is as simple
as love.
Listen to love.
Let it guide
each moment
because that
is all there is.
Love and this moment.
Be patient
humble
present
Let love unfold and
take its course.
BE. LOVE!

1/18/15 9:27am

there's a reason
for
everythingeachpersoneachmoment
why some strangers
look like us
so we can see
ourselvesfamilyfriends
in each person.
Each moment
we live
is love
a miracle.
Fear wants me
to rushpanicfallcrash
Not this time.
People are miracles
just as nature is.
We are part of nature.
We are part of this world.
We are part of each other.
We are not apart.
We are together.
We are connected.
We are alive
We are LOVE!

BE. LOVE!

1/18/15 1:13pm

Resting and enjoying
the breeze
that continues
despite all the pavement
in this parking lot.
I am human.
I am an addict.
I am an alcoholic.
I am a scared little boy.
I am my ego
Only when I choose to.
Be.
I am not my ego.
My ego is a part
of my mind
I choose to hold onto.
Ego is fear.
I choose to let go
I choose to be
whole
love
not just apart
a part
a number
a label
a criminal.
I am human.
I need help.
I need love.

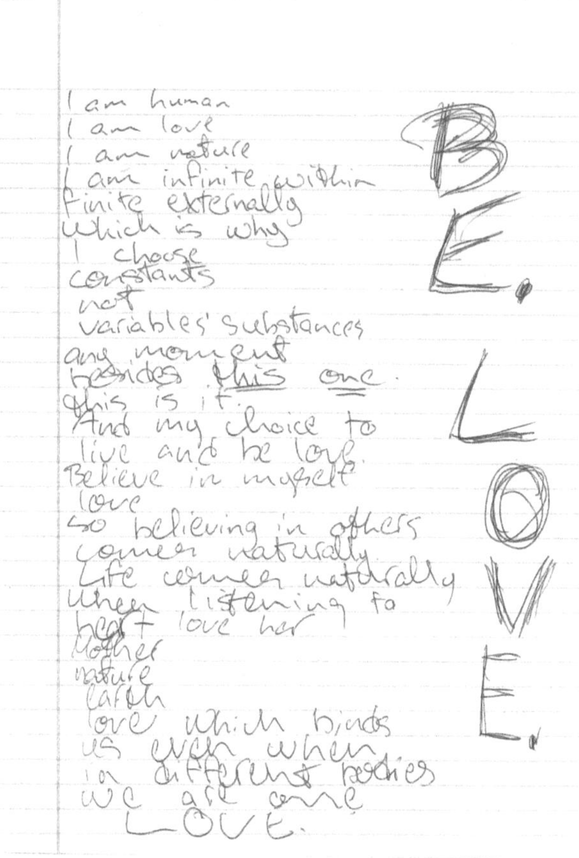


I am human
I am love
I am nature
I am infinite within
finite externally
Which is why
I choose
constants
not
variables' substances
any moment
besides this one.
This is it.
And my choice to
live and be love.
Believe in myself
love
So believing in others
comes naturally.
Life comes naturally
When listening to
heart love her
Mother
nature
Earth
love which binds
us even when
in different bodies
we are one
LOVE.

Love needs
nothing
but us to choose
We get to choose?
LOVE!
How beautiful
what a blessing
life is
nature is
love is
humanity is
choice is
We get to walk
our own
path
All paths lead
to love
even when fear
takes hold
We choose to
let go
and forge
ahead
courageously
lovingly
we protect chunks of
metalglassscreenscars
instead of love nature home us
Let go!!!
BE! LOVE!

This body is a vessel.
I am blessed and grateful.
Focus
        on
            the
                space
            because
        Life
            is
    A
        DANCE
So enjoy it! Explore!
        We
            are
                astronauts
        Flying through love's space.
Every space
            is
                there
        to create
            in
                LOVE!
Nature is love
and continues to grow
So do we
Must learn to
    love
            the
                process ➞ LIFE!

Trust
love
Resist
temptation
We can choose love
SO WE MUST
Be
both
Hornet
and
Honeybee
Life is
balance.
Life is
practice.
Life is
courage to do what is right
Life is
patience to drop what is left
Life is
baby steps
Life is
choice in stepping
forward →
not
← backwards
Life is
Continuity
when we love
see what happens next!

Breathe
and
BE
present
BE
LOVE
Do not call
on the past
to solve the
present
Just BE!
Love is present
Love is life
Love is the blueprint
Love is listening
Love is sharing
Love is.
Be fierce
as a hornet
BE humble
as a honeybee
Be LOVE
Love is all
of us
all of
nature
everything
No need to label or speak
Just be present. Be in awe
BE. LOVE.

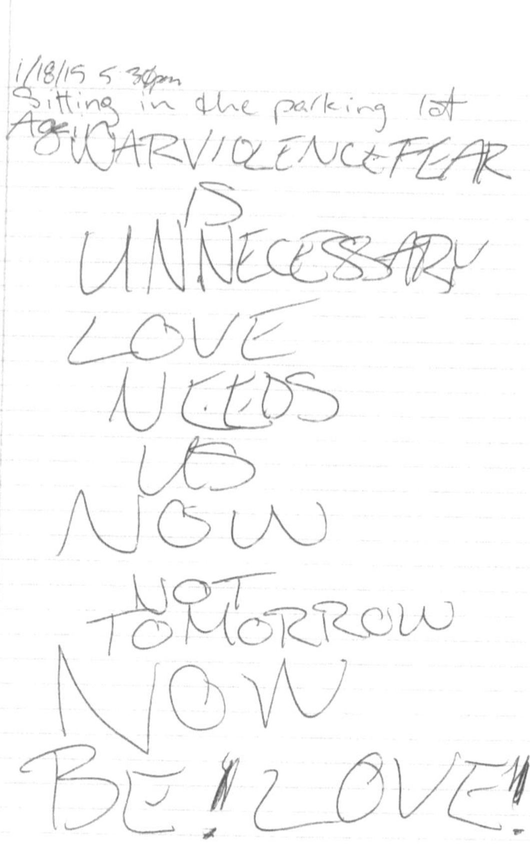
1/18/15 5:30pm
Sitting in the parking lot
WAR VIOLENCE FEAR
IS
UNNECESSARY
LOVE
NEEDS
US
NOW
NOT TOMORROW
NOW
BE!! LOVE!!

1/18/15 7:42pm
Along for
the ride
Life is
found in
these moments
this moment
New friends
Dear friends
don't need filters
fear.
We are love
We are life
We are this
very
moment
Movies arcades adventures
Seeing where the night
goes,
We go with the moment
To the hills.
Let's find a view
Let's be with nature
Let's be together.
Lean trust in trust
Filters are fear.
Life is holding on
and letting go of
each moment.
stay present
BE LOVE

No need to worry
these are friends
Not just people.
We are alive
We do not need
   to drink smoke use
JUST BE
here we ARE
this moment
   is it
LIFE!
Who knows
where the road leads
we do not
We do not need to
LOVE knows
     ALL
Just listen
the moment
speaks for itself
Let love unfold
and take the wheel
let the past cycle
We do not need
anything
   but
      this
BE! LOVE! moment!

1/18/15 8:48pm
Here
WE
ARE
On top of
the
world
this
city
this
hill
this
moment
this
breeze
is
as
clean
as
IN THIS us
MOMENT
San Jose
is
beautiful
We are San Jose
WE ARE solace valley

From up here
the view
this city
this moment
this valley
this hill
It is all
LOVE
So much to take in
the lights!
the clouds!
the stars!
the sounds!
the animals call
the breeze calls
the moment calls
US
TO
LOVE
RIGHT
NOW

We are light
Feel the light
coursing guiding loving
Feel each and every
All that has
presence
present! connect!
BEAUTIFUL! It's LOVE!

1/19/15 5:44pm a.m.

Here we are!
   Alive! Again!
Another day to
   be grateful for.
Every moment
   we spend with
   our fellows
   rather than
   turning against
   another, brother/sister/mother/father
   is a blessing
   and step
   forward
We need every son and daughter
   moving
   forward ———>!!!
We need every son and daughter
   moving away from fear!
We need every son and daughter
   to guide their scared
   parents/grandparents/friends/family
   with action!
   By leading!
   By loving!
   Our love
   Our nonviolence
   Our choice
      NOW!!!
   BE! LOVE!

We have this moment
We have this opportunity
to
U-TURN
HISTORY
ON THE FREEWAY
BY SIMPLY
LIVING AND
CHOOSING
TO WALK
INSTEAD OF
DRIVE
Live in steps
→ Not the
fast lane
The fast lane
leads to a brick fucking wall

We can choose to change
We can choose a different
    of course
It's easy! To U-Turn
    and choose!
      LOVE!
Turn away from fear/violence/substance
  LOVE is everywhere
  LOVE is all
      When we listen
Let go of fear
      It's never done us good
Time to rewrite history
Time to write history
Time to write love
Time to BE LOVE!!!
Time to live! Time to dance!
      Time
          to
              celebrate!
We are the example.
Melt our fear
Melt our weapons
Hug our "enemies"
Hug our selfs
Hug ourselves
      TOGETHER! BE! LOVE!!

Only when we drop
EGO
OUR OWN FIRST
Can we learn by example
We are at war with ourselves
NOT EACH OTHER

Our enemy is US

Our enemy is FEAR

Our answer is LOVE!

Quite simple to see
Quite simple to hear
Quite simple to feel
Quite simple to be
Quite simple to love
Quite simple to live
We complicate
life
When we stop
When we turn against
When we fear
LOVE
BE! LOVE!

7:14am
When we know we don't know
When we know we are scared
When we know we need help
We know we need nothing
When we know this
When we know fear
We know ego
When we know our ego
We can choose
We can ignore the ego
We can listen to our heart
We can listen to each other
We can see each other
We can see our friends
family
ourselves

When we see ourselves in each
When we see
We know
We are
We love
We live
Our fears live in our mind
Our fear lives within
SO DOES LOVE
I CHOOSE LOVE
ABANDON FEAR
LET LOVE GROW
BE! LOVE!

Our dreams are the last battlefield
Our fear is our last enemy.
Our    Filters distractions
            substances
            screens
            walls
            buildings towers storefronts
Are only temporary
       Our bodies are temporary
   OUR LOVE IS ETERNAL

We are eternal
       Our spirit
            soul
            identity
            LOVE
                IS

                    ETERNAL
INFINITE
WE ARE STARS
WE ARE LOVE
     BE! LOVE!

7:24am
It is happening
This is happening
Not tomorrow
NOT YESTERDAY
TODAY
RIGHT NOW
this moment
LOVE
triumphs
Love carries us
We must choose to
LET GO
AND
LET LOVE
SHINE

When we are clean
we are brighter than ever
we are the example
we light the world
we love the world
we love ourselves
we love each other
we love nature
We LOVE
LIVE
BE! LOVE!

7:28am
Two minutes
  Two is enough
    this is enough
Each moment exists
  We exist
    FOR A REASON
      LOVE

Choose love in each moment
Do not think
Let go and let love
Love connects us
  We are love

11:04am

the hand, body, mind
    SHAKE & TREMBLE
  when we want to
    give in
    give up
WE MUST KEEP
    LOVE
      ALIVE
This moment is important
  because I am
    STILL HERE

LOVE
IS
ALL
WE
ARE
LOVE!

EXHALE_

CHAPTER THIRTY_

Tuesday 9/28/15 10:46pm

I'm still scared. No matter how far into recovery I've made it, the truth remains. I'm petrified of tomorrow. I keep making progress, but then I slide into days into weeks of sloth. I'm scared of failure. I'm scared of success. I'm scared to move. I'm scared of standing still. My body & mind tremble through each moment of each passing day. Even w/ a brighter tomorrow than ever before, I can't help but feel it's all going to come crashing down. that I'll unravel b/c I'm not worth it despite constantly mounting proof otherwise.

My stomach aches w/ guilt of harm done to others & myself. Shamed w/ a life of missed opportunities & squandered potential. I live in the shadow of myself, of what could & should be, but never will. I'm exhausted carrying this burden: me. I can't stand myself. I hate mirrors, getting my photo taken, any visible proof that I exist. I just want to dissappear w/ a quick dissolving fade out.

As long as I can remember, I've been my own worst enemy. In constant battle w/ just getting out of bed in the morning & facing the day. I just want to hide & be alone, away from anyone who can see me, including myself. this body has been & continues to be my prison. No matter what I've done to help my self-image, I still loathe the sight of ~~myself~~. me

Each attempt to better myself only ends up magnifying my dysphoria. Growing a beard for a couple years, working out religiously & reaching the best shape of my life, getting tattoos to cover my hideously rough skin, it's all just distractions. Distractions that become increasingly difficult to hide behind w/ each day I remain clean & sober. I threw away the efforts I've made to better my body. I eat too much & have put all the weight back on & then some. I spend too much ~~&~~ on cigarettes & dumb stuff so I don't have enough to get more tattoos I know would make me happier.

I finally shaved my beard last week, exactly one week ago, ~~the~~ Not for the job interview I had the following day, but b/c I couldn't fall for my own lies anymore. I told myself it was to get a job → lie. I told myself the beard would make me more masculine & proud → lie. I told myself I'd meet the real me by growing out the beard → LIE.

I met the real me when I shaved my beard & saw through all my lies. I was vulnerable, naked, broken from 24 years spent trying to believe the front I was putting on for the rest of the world. Only in trying to live for them, I was killing myself from the inside out.

Staring at my reflection this time was different. I saw right through the scared little boy staring back at me. I saw through to the scared little girl who's been here as long as I can remember, my whole life. Scared her sentence in this body's prison would be a lifetime. Scared her story would never be told, that no one would care or love her. Scared that she wasn't deserving of love & would spend her life peering out of male eyes to a world where people got their happily ever afters. Everyone but her.

I smiled at her, hugged her w/ my eyes as they swelled w/ tears, & knew immediately in my heart of hearts is my truth that scared little girl is me. I've spent my life trying to ignore who I am on the inside, resigning that it would never match my outside yet running myself into the ground trying anyways. The time for running is over. I'll never be able to outrun myself, my core, my truth, who I really am.

I am transgender.
I have a voice.
I am worth loving.
My life is worth living.
My life is deserving of joy.
Tomorrow is worth waking up for.

I refuse to believe my old, scared, tired lies. This past week has been the brightest of my life. It's still not easy, having my body reflect my burden, but I finally see & love the me hiding underneath & know her time to shine is closer than ever before.

Thursday October 15, 2015 10:55pm

    I spend my days teetering on the edge, always a moment away from bursting into tears. Years spent living for others, refusing to acknowledge the beautiful girl trapped within male skin, I'm seeing it was all a waste of effort. I'm so tired of the exhaustion I put myself through to try & assimilate. I'm tired of hating myself. I'm tired of pushing the world away from me, I am absolutely sick of the dark cloud I've forced myself to live under. I'm cold, weak, scared, lonely, & drenched to the bone from my own tears. Petrified I'd never be able to love myself & in turn those around me.

    Today I am nine months clean. It's been more than a year since my last drink. I have finally seen a glimpse of the real me hiding behind these sad eyes. I am just so damn scared. I'm scared of letting the real me rise out of the ashes of my past. I'm scared to be really seen when I've spent my whole life hiding or running. I'm scared of abandoning my old defense mechanisms & letting my walls come down. I'm scared of the unknown. Which is truly conflicting.

    I know the known way of living to this point has only caused me more pain. I know at my core that the unknown is where I find serenity, joy, & love. I'm just having the damndest time retraining my muscle memory. I know this transition is my path. I know this path is setting me free. Yet I still panic & worry more about what others think rather than what brings me peace.

Tonight I didn't even feel safe at a meeting. The secretary kept asking & trying to remember my dead name. Even the chairperson stood up for me, telling the secretary she shouldn't be asking. Yet I still cave & tell her, feeling awful even saying that name out loud. Even when I know it's a safe place & others are standing up for me, I still have trouble standing up for myself. So naturally when called on to share, I only skim the surface & withhold my truth. I choose to see only the cis hetero guys in the room. I choose to ignore my friend in the room. She's been a rock through this. Yet I choose to panic. I choose to let the men scare me & keep me from being honest. I choose to judge them & react before they can judge me. Then I sit in my own misery the rest of the meeting. Why do I keep choosing old behaviors & negativity?

There are so many wonderful positives happening every day now. I need to focus on those and keep the momentum heading forward. I've already come too far to risk throwing everything good away. It feels indescribable to hear a room echo my true name when I introduce myself at a meeting. It feels just as good having my friend there for me after the meeting. I loved listening to what's been on her mind this week & then be able to be completely honest about my fears.

She understands without having to know exactly what this journey feels like. Her hug meant the world tonight. On a funny note, of course the Billie Eilish's "Afraid of Everyone" came on while writing this paragraph.

Today really was a beautiful day. I was up early enough to enjoy the chilly & cloudy morning. I made a dent in an assignment for a company I'd like to interview & work at based in SF. I didn't panic when I knew I couldn't finish it today. And there's awesome AWESOME news! I made an appointment with a doctor in Santa Cruz, so I can hopefully start HRT soon! The bad news: it's not till mid-November. Of course I dwell on the wait instead of focusing on the positive: it's all <u>happening</u>. Need to remember it's my Higher Power's timeline, not mine. I'm just so giddy & excited at the thought of HRT, I can hardly wait. Also looks like my face is healing well from the first electrolysis appointment I had yesterday. Life is really looking up, so it's no use looking down or behind me. Eyes to the horizon!
And one more thing...
this girl has a name.

Love,
Mackenzie

Tuesday 11/17/15 9:35pm

Being human cracks me up. An imperfect creature striving for a demanding perfection from life. I'm able to recognize life is perfect the way it is otherwise it'd be different. I can recognize I'm where I need to be, but feeling & recognizing are different from each other. I know I'm on the right path, but I keep having difficulty holding onto faith. I keep living in fear to the point of freezing in place.

Even now I'm dancing around w/ words b/c I'm scared of truly being honest. I'm scared of someone else seeing the real me. I'm scared of putting myself - my heart - on paper & having the person reading crumple me up, cast me aside, or set me ablaze just to watch me burn.

The truth is that as scary as that is, this constant pain of hiding & resigning to a defeated life is indescribably worse. Most days I try & hide within my skin & numb myself with negative thoughts to avoid any real relationships with those around me. Having the world see Morgan instead of Mackenzie on a daily basis is an exhausting & agonizing state. I'm tired of playing the part of sixtrouman to strangers. I'm tired of explaining why questions about surgery are personal to people I barely know. I'm tired of being patient with family misgendering me. I'm absolutely sickened that a place as dumb as a bathroom is the frontline of the gender battleground. If I use the correct one, I'm looked at as a predator & I feel like absolute filth using the one society wants me to. Can't a girl just take a piss in peace?

Tues. Dec. 8, 2015 11:55pm

I need to keep writing. I need to keep walking forward instead of fearfully stalling. The turmoil of negative energy around me is always going to be there. Lately its creeps pulling at my skirt, tweaker neighbors acting erratically, my dad's drinking increase, & my own ego trying to sabotage my progress. My instinct is to give in & meet negativity w/ even more. My instinct is to skip Christmas in Southern California & hide from the stares, gossip & inane trans questions about what's between my legs. Then again, my instinct's also to smoke a forest of pot to numb myself in self-pity. Look where that got me. If I have the opportunity to help someone, it's my obligation to.

The best things in my life have only come after hard work or sacrifice. Every event has happened for a reason & led me here. The louder the negativity, the more I need to focus b/c it's a sign something good's around the corner. It'll be good to go down south. Sure, there's going to be some awkward conversations. I'm ready for them. I love who I am. I love Mackenzie. I don't need to defend myself b/c I'm in a beautiful place which only gets brighter w/ each day.

I'm still reeling from Sunday night seeing The Weeknd at the Shark Tank. It was my sixth time seeing him since 2012, but my first time sober & as the real me. I went alone & the crowd only cared about his new album, but I had a blast & looked cute as well. Abel was as great as he's always been. The way he lives in the moment & always strives to improve is inspiring.

January 16, 2016

"Hᴜᴛ ᴜᴛ!" I yell ahead. Within moments I'm up out of the water gliding on Lake Don Pedro. I wipe my face with one hand while the other's holding onto the rope. Grinning from ear to ear I take in the moment and surroundings.

I can't believe it's all happening. Here I am, one year (and a day) sober, wakeboarding on the lake I practically grew up on. I've embraced my skeleton form and don't need to hide who I am anymore. I smile up to the cloudless sky in gratitude, then shift focus to the boat pulling me.

Dad's driving, wearing his lake-staple train conductor hat. Madison's sitting next to him and flashes me a smile and wave. Hudson's in his lap grinning and barking ecstatically. Against Me!'s "Transgender Dysphoria Blues" blasts from the boat's speakers, fueling my run.

I signal to Madison a thumb up which he relays to Dad. The rope tightens as does my grip on the handle. With a little more speed, I'm able to find my groove and start carving back and forth across the wake. Water sprays up with each pass and glistens in the sunlight.

Wait a sec, it's not just the light off the water shimmering. I glance down at myself and witness the impossible. My bones shine and shimmer brighter than the water. My eyes fill with tears of joy. Joy for the chance to celebrate as the real me with my family. The tears stream down me and wash away to reveal a fresh layer of skin peeking out from my wetsuit.

Madison stares from the boat and shakes Dad's shoulder without shifting his gaze. Dad glances back to see what's going on and drops his jaw accordingly. They high-five each other and shake their hands up to their sister and daughter at the other end of the rope.

Their celebratory tears fall to Hudson who shakes out in Madison's lap to reveal a fresh coat of fur. He barks several more times and spins around to plant some kisses on Madison. I smile through tears and look on at the family. They finally see the real me. And Hudson's back too.

We continue along the lake as I watch the hills and passing coves from behind the boat. "It's time. She's ready," a voice passes by me. "Are you sure? They're not to be trusted," a second voice replies. "I trust her," the first responds. I look ahead to the boat and yell to my family, but they can't hear me. Then who and what did I just hear? I look up to the tree-line of a passing hill and see a patch of rustling bushes. It was probably just the wind. Before I can even finish another thought to myself, a grizzly bear emerges from the foliage and stares directly at me – through me.

I lose control of the wakeboard, face plant into the water, and let go of the rope. When I emerge, the bear's long gone and the boat circles back to pick me up. "What happened out there, Mackenzie? You looked like you saw a ghost before you bailed," Madison asks as I climb into the boat. "Yeah, something like that," I mutter and take a seat with Hudson. I don't take my eyes off the hills the rest of the trip back to our campsite.

DUSK THAT EVENING.

Following dinner, I notice a firefly hovering around me while I clean my dishes. The light darts around me quicker and brighter than any insect. Chills run down my arms as I realize it's not a bug at all. I pause and meditate in order to hear the light's message. "Hello! We love you! It's time! Follow!" it sings playfully. The light spirals around Hudson and me once more before darting to the family's boat at the shore nearby. I look over to Dad and Madison finishing their meal and watching the sunset. They don't seem to notice the light or hear it.

"Hey Dad, would it be cool to take Hudson out on the water to get some time together?" I call over to him. "Sure, but don't be too long. The sun's going down and I want to make sure you can find your way back," he replies. "Sure thing, I just need to clear my mind a bit. Thanks," I assure him as he tosses me the keys to the boat. Hudson jumps at me grinning and turns to chase the light to the boat.

As I reach the boat, Hudson jumps into my arms and squirms his way onboard. I hear him bark excitedly, running the length of the boat. I push us off the shore and climb in. I immediately fall into the seat of the open bow and stare at Hudson. He's surrounded in tiny wisps of light, jumping and playing with them. He catches my stare, looks directly at me, and grinningly projects, "Hi Mackenzie! It's ok! They're friends!" I smile back as Hudson runs over and jumps in my lap. The lights now dance and circle around us. I'm fully at peace and can hear them sing, "Let's go! Much to see! We love you! Come! Follow!" They fill the boat with light and make their way in front of us, hovering over the water and lighting a path. I hop back to the driver's seat and bring the boat up to speed while Hudson looks ahead from his perch at the bow.

We follow the swirling path of light past several coves before the singing picks up again. "Almost there! So close! Just you wait! Almost there!" the lights continue on. The next cove approaches. The shining trail curves in and speeds off towards a bubbling circle of light tucked away close to the shore.

I cut the engine and drop anchor at the entrance to the cove. Hudson's barks subside to steady whimpers and pants. I join him at the bow and look toward the circle of light and the shore. I sharpen my focus to make out the shadowy figure by the water's edge. My eyes widen and jaw drops as the figure gets closer to the water's light.

Despite never seeing any wildlife at the lake in all my years besides fish and birds, here's the same grizzly as earlier today. The bear's coat shines when any light catches it. I look on as the bear approaches the water, casually rises upright on its hind legs, looks over at us, and walks into the water towards the light until it sinks out of view.

Hudson and I look at each other with a collective sigh and jump into the lake. We swim along the path to the still bubbling circle of light. As we approach the edge of the circle, the water's temperature steadily rises, though not hot – comfortable. The bubbling subsides; I take a deep breath, and dive under.

Below the surface a tunnel of dancing, shimmering light descends from the surface's circle to the bottom of the lake. Normally I'd not be able to see two feet in any direction under this lake, but the tunnel illuminates a clear shot to a shining dome at the lake's floor. The dome and floor look far deeper than I know this lake to be. No matter, we've got to catch that bear and make sense of this.

Hudson joins me in the light's tunnel under the surface and we push deeper. The tunnel shifts its size to match its passengers. We continue our journey, bear in sight. I look behind us and find we're far deeper than I thought. The circle disappears from the surface and the tunnel quickly closes in behind us. I panic in fear of drowning, but realize I can breathe while in the tunnel. Hudson doesn't seem to notice at all.

"I am here. Follow me," the voice from earlier returns. I look ahead and watch the grizzly reach the dome. The bear passes through without any resistance.

Hudson and I swim deeper and meet the outside of the dome. Without a second thought, Hudson projects, "Trust your heart, not your mind," and leaps into the dome. With both Hudson and the bear out of sight, I take a final breath and dive through the dome's wall.

Once I cross over, my eyes widen as though I've just seen the most beautiful sight of my life. My eyes swell with tears and my ears are greeted with the happiest bark I've ever heard.

ACKNOWLEDGMENTS_

To Mom, Hudson, my friends & family who stuck around, and those who connect with this work: thank you for saving my life.

We are never alone.

Mackenzie Parsons is an emerging author who lives in Oakland, California with her companion, Hudson. This is Mackenzie's first book.

If you enjoyed this piece of work, please consider taking a few minutes to leave a review on Amazon. It's one of the best ways to help indie authors.